HER DARK SOUL

DARK SPELL SERIES BOOK 5

ISRA SRAVENHEART

CONTENTS

DEDICATION

Because of you, this work was finished despite many troublesome things along the way.

You are the reason I didn't give up and finished writing it.

It is because of you that Her Dark Soul is now in print.

Thank you for everything!

A NOTE FOR MY READERS

The Dark Spell Series *was written starting with*
Her Dark Soul,
following with Heart, Rose, *and then I wrote* Dark Love *and* Kissing
Darkness.
So as far as series order goes, this comes after
Queen of Darkness.
I've given this a more fitting re-write too so that we get right back to where
Queen of Darkness *leaves off.*

Yes, I know I did a George Lucas here and considering I wrote Seducing
Darkness, Queen of Darkness, *and* Darkness Reborn *in 2021, which
are respectively books 3, 4, and 8 in the series, I've had to do a fair amount
of shifting things around so it isn't confusing to my readers.*

Anyhoo, enjoy!

PROLOGUE

Samuel had just gotten back to Spirisity. It hadn't been very far considering he'd just clicked his thumb and index finger together after he'd left Isra comatose in Shambre Fell. The place he had planned for her to be after he'd disarmed her for the second time and was now preparing for the next steps. With Astrid also gone and out of the way. Samuel had assumed he'd have flown off somewhere licking his wounds no doubt, but he was unharmed and free to do as he pleased just as long as it didn't involve Isra.

Well, it's been a busy day. One could say I have definitely earned this coffee. Samuel marvelled to himself as it had just approached seven o'clock in the morning. Of course, Wretchenheart castle had burned to its very last cinders after Samuel had gotten out of there with Isra in tow. He wanted to ensure that nobody of Isra's magnitude could hide out in there again. So, killing two birds with one stone. Wretchenheart had long been the habitual locale for many witches and warlocks escaping the light and it had been well and truly time to put a stop to that. After all, someone else would only have shacked up in there if Isra wasn't still holed up in there herself. *It is what it is. Astrid would have gotten out. I know he did. I didn't see him but, in any event, I am certain he would have managed to skedalle. It would have a damn failure on my part if he had succumbed to death as a result of such a calamity. Ah needs must. What is a fella to do when a witch won't listen to reason? On high, sorry the real one, The Sanctification of the Unseen instructed me that I must take Isra down by whatever means necessary and I have done so. I cannot change it now all that awaits us is what we must do after this. That is what counts.* Samuel continued mulling over it all in his thoughts just as he presumed that a hot coffee could be just the ticket after the gruelling night and morning he'd had.

"Is it done then?" James asked with a look of interest. The mousy brown-haired man had just poked his head around the door of Samuel's office as he strode in without a care.

"Yes, it is. She's back at Shambre Fell under my sleeping spell until I decide what the best move will be for her." Samuel mouthed, stifling a yawn. He was tired. It had been a long night, but light-bringers often went without sleep for weeks and even months at a time. He would handle it as efficiently as he could. There was no immediate cause for alarm right now.

"But they have intended for her to be incarcerated here in Spirisity have they not?" James narrowed his eyes at Samuel with immense scrutiny. Surely the light-bringer wouldn't be so bold as to deny a direct order from the real folks in charge yet again? That would be really scraping the barrel wouldn't it?

"That's what they are wanting to commence. Yes. However how would we even begin to know what to do with her? Sure, the basement level of this unique chateau would provide the perfect domicile for our Lady Isra of the Dark but how would one keep her there with due restraints?" Samuel asked James the question in a cordial fashion.

Spirisity did have its unique dungeon, but it had not been used for a considerable time. Since Samuel had occupied the property two hundred years ago, he had not took it upon himself to care for the neglected prison cell that would have housed many witches like Isra once upon a time. Back in the days, when witches like Isra was unfairly crucified. And some were burned alive so that their rotten magic died along with them. It was a rather extreme methodology in which the light handled witches but those were the times that had befallen us. But of course, it was fair to say, those times were long dead. Samuel didn't believe in those methods. Neither did he want to lay claim to them. It was a fruitless endaevour. One that he felt didn't actually get to the root issue of why someone would explore their darker side of their soul in the first place.

"Any chance of a coffee James? I am parched." Samuel requested with eagerness as he considered a plausible idea that while it would be against the real on high's wishes it may just work.

"Of course." James narrowed his eyes at Samuel wondering what the light-bringer was up to. He seemed awfully quiet for someone who had just done the unthinkable in order to attain the impossible.

"Thank you, old chap," Samuel responded curtly before he turned his attention to his thoughts once more.

What if we constructed false memories of her attaining her title of Lady Isra of the Dark and just kept her in Shambre Fell? Isra knows she has turned the tide and that will remain so. She won't forget that whole debacle with Jonathan or Everilda for that matter. Neither will she be able to let slip from her mind of how she gave her heart up to the darkness but what if we did a rewrite on the girl's head? So that she's still the powerful formidable force everyone made her out to be but she's having to start anew knowing that was some kind of trouble.

What if I took it upon myself to create that? Yes, a whole new way of existing. She'd be intact and nobody would be any the wiser. Spirisity and everyone in it could be cloaked until the time came whereby, we'd have to step in because eventually Astrid will find his way back to her. He always does. In any event, that sounds like it's the best solution to a very complex problem. I don't have the mental capacity to house her here. Where would I even start in relation to rehabilitating her? It seems foolish especially as I have already taken her memories. She'd never take to me or pay any mind to anything I said, not like this. I'd just appear as some pompous know it all; her elder that has already attempted to chatasise her a hundred times. No, it won't work that way. I already know it.

I can't bank on Astrid not making a reappearance at some stage of the juncture but that's not my concern right now. All I have to do is convince on high that I've done my utmost to ensure she's out of harm's way. Nobody would ever guess that this is done by my design. I could build walls around Isra that even she wouldn't dare try to tear down. It would become impossible for her to become close to another because unless she opens her heart and someone manages to break through they'd be damned anyhow. Samuel chorused in thought as he seemed to have it all planned out. He'd leave Isra as she was but just make a few adjustments along the way.

"And thus emerges our new way of being." Samuel uttered profoundly as James entered the office carrying two steaming mugs of coffee and a bar of chocolate to share. Even those working in the light needed a sugar hit from time to time.

So, what had become to Astrid, you say? Well, let's just say our plucky raven wasn't harmed in the fiery flames at Wretchenheart but he did assume that it was the light-bringer's intent to kill him. Why wouldn't Astrid think that? He knew just how powerful his connection with Isra was and because Samuel was deeply threatened by Isra and with Astrid standing right by her side, well quite frankly Astrid felt he was in the way of a grand kerfuffle.

Astrid had seen for himself the grim side of Samuel Reynaldi and so he wasn't going to waste any time convincing anyone otherwise but after a while nearly everyone gets corrupted, don't they? It's the human condition. And sure, Samuel Reynaldi couldn't attest to such a fact but it remained the same. He was affected deeply by the job at hand, and he couldn't control his emotions to it. Not anymore. It was sad but Astrid felt there was nothing he could do. As far as he was aware, there was a prophecy involving Isra and a sordid black rose however Astrid didn't know when it would emerge and only then could he return to his beloved. But in the meantime, he'd just keep watch on her from a safe distance because you know he truly could not let Isra go.

"I can't change anything that's happened." Astrid summarised as he took one more look at the beaten relic that used to be Wretchenheart castle. When Samuel had magically disarmed Isra for the second time, he'd bloody burned the damn place down after all he'd imbued himself with demon blood so he could enter otherwise he wouldn't have had a prayer. But never mind let's forget for one moment the light-bringer's deviousness and focus on the man of the hour.

Astrid had gone back to Shambre Fell to keep an eye on Isra who was knee deep in a comatose sleep. She looked almost peaceful as she laid there unaware of any of the chaotic events that had occured in the last few days. To think that Astrid had not only been with Isra, devoured her and lost her all in the space of forty-eight hours it didn't seem real. But it was. He was there.

"I'm not entirely sure on how to get back to you." Astrid retorted from where he was sat on Isra's window ledge. "It's not an easy feat. We accomplished so much and to fall at the wayside like this at the last hurdle well it doesn't bear thinking about. I'll have to work harder this time. I'll find a way. I don't know how and in the meantime all I have is time. So many long-lost years until I can hold you in my arms again."

Astrid was trying his utmost not to think of his loss. It was too much to bear but he wasn't going anywhere either.... He'd often sit on the window ledge of Shambre Fell unaware of what was happening back in Spirisity. Where the light-bringer was yet again wheedling another plan.

"Ah not brilliant but it will do." Samuel marvelled to himself as he looked back at the sleeping image of Isra laying on her bed while he stood a few inches away from her. If he was even more intelligent, he'd have noticed the black raven perched on the edge of the window ledge watching Samuel's every move but alas he did not.

"Well, I best be off. I have to take care of Spirisity too. James won't like it but I will just send him on an extended vacation. The boy could do with a break. The last three years really has been a great ordeal for all of us." Samuel remarked coyly. He'd done what he'd set out to do and that was by creating a new set of memories for Isra however Samuel was the only one who knew what those memories were. Astrid didn't have the foggiest as he watched Samuel disappear into a puff of smoke but one thing was certain, he'd be around a lot more now since the heat was definitely off.

Astrid didn't care too much for the fact that Samuel was going to take care of Spirisity. *Whatever the hell that means but knowing him who dares to know?? It's not going to be great but it's okay as Oresis said one day Samuel Reynaldi's folly will be exposed and that is when all of us can rest safely in the knowing that we all played a part in his fall. In the meantime, I'll just sit back, munch on a few worms and watch over my precious Isra. Maybe I'll teach her a thing or two as she goes alone on her journey. But yet she won't be will she?* Astrid chuckled to himself in thought with a wink still watching his sleeping lover from afar.

1

From the beginning, there has always been magic. It can destroy us, but it can also be the best thing for us. Things are not always black and white; witches are not always bad, but they are not always good, either.

Back to a time not so long ago, there was a witch named Lady Isra, and she was incredibly powerful. She possessed many abilities and qualities: power, control, authority, and beauty. But yet she had no heart, and a witch without a heart is a wicked witch indeed because, as this story tells, she became darker as time went on.

We began in autumn when the leaves were tumbling down from the trees in bold shades of cherry, flamed orange, and burnt copper. The land was changing; the season of summer was escaping. Many men and women cared not to dwell here because the witch that lived in the desolate tower in Shambre Fell was one sure to be cautious of.

Amidst the beauty of the land, a majestic shining tower stood on a hilltop and was the center of it all, showcasing the land's most ferocious villain. Lady Isra of the Dark. She was not at all kind, graceful, or loving. She had lost love many years ago, and now only bitter tears flowed. Tears of what she had lost, tears of what she'd once had. Tears of fear, regret, and pain because young loves dream had not turned out to be what she had envisioned. It was a sad tragic loss but that aside the plucky light-bringer had engineered it so that Isra still felt that heartbreak from the weasel Jonathan however she was led to believe she had attained her title Lady Isra of the Dark because of him when in actual fact she had not done so.

Life for this witch was never quite the same as it once was. She kept to herself and spoke with only the animals, having a strong connection with them. Isra admired their beauty and power. She knew many of the beings by name, and some were even guides and messengers who helped her from time to time. They were not afraid of her, despite the consuming darkness inside her soul. They saw good in all beings, a trait not very well known. It was also well documented that a jet-black raven often toddled alongside Isra on her travels but keeping out of sight just enough so that Isra would be none the wiser.

In this land, the witch was respected but also feared. It was said in many villages, "Do not cross the witch! She is villainous and doesn't take kindly to being crossed." The best advice the townspeople could give was, "Stay away from her." but they were not aware of her history. I doubt they'd have cared about all of the heartache she'd received when she had gotten here to Shambre Fell. People were quick to judge, well Isra knew that.

The witch did not care for them or their words; she lived in seclusion and had done so for most of her life and was comfortable with it. She spent most of her time studying her craft and learning more about the world she lived in, reading up on all the secret and not so secret knowledge of the magical world that few knew of or even cared about.

Sometimes people would come to the witch because they'd heard of the things she could do. She could banish, but she could bind and return selfish and negative behaviors back to those who had originally cast them out, as well. She knew every curse and all the hexes. If someone had a problem and wasn't afraid of her, she was the one they could go to for help. Isra was a formidable force to be reckoned with and if one could swallow their pride and let go of that impenetrable fear she might just resolve their issue altogether even if the idea of it send shivers down their spine.

A young lady had come to the witch and asked for her help, for another woman was attempting to take her husband. The witch prepared a spell, and after doing everything that needed to be done, she sat the young woman down and told her what to do. When they were done, she thought it was the last she would hear from her. But sometimes even with the most proficient of magic spells this isn't always the case. Spells have a tendency to either backfire or, in this case, not perform as well as to be expected. Sometimes the target resists the magical pull and that can cause the person who asked Lady Isra of the Dark to cast the spell anguish, but Isra knew it was part of the course. Humans don't always respond well to others so how do you expect them to respond well to an enchantment placed upon them? Exactly!

A week later, on a full moon, the young woman contacted the witch again. Isra had been sitting at her table sorting herbs and putting them into their correctly labeled jars when a loud knock on the old, stiff oak door startled her whilst she was upstairs in her living room. Isra waited for a moment as the heard knock sound again before she ran down the gray stone staircase only to see it was the young woman once more.

Isra stared the young woman awkwardly in the face. Her eyes were filled to the brim with tears. She had most definitely been crying. *Pardon me to say it but if you cry over a man. Oh, golly.* Isra gushed to herself as she too had been in this predicament and knew that crying over some foolish imbecile got you nowhere.

"He's going to leave me for her!" the young woman cried.

"Yes, I am sure he is. Calm down and come upstairs. I will make some tea, dear." Isra replied solemnly. You must understand Isra wasn't mocking the young woman, but she knew how these situations played out. Sometimes they worked immediately and then not so much. This was displaying much of the latter.

Isra led the young woman into her home and invited her to sit down on her couch.

Isra then went into the kitchenette and grabbed a dagger. She asked the young woman to hold out her hand. The woman did as Isra requested. The witch carefully slashed the dagger across the young woman's hand, making an incision just below the young woman's marriage finger. Isra paused before she let the thick, red blood drip onto a piece of parchment and then into a cup of water.

"Write his name on the parchment. And drink the water. This will bind him to you and only you. It has never failed me," said the witch in a soft tone. Of course, it wasn't a situation Isra could personally speak of its success. She had never beguiled her lover Jonathan and if she had well perhaps, she wouldn't be where she was now but it never does one any good to dwell on these things.

The young woman wrote her husband's name on the parchment and gave it back to the witch, who folded it in halves a few times, then wrapped string tightly around the parcel. She handed it to the young woman.

"Now place this somewhere hidden, close to where he sleeps. Go, you must do this immediately!"

And with that, Isra never heard from the young woman again.

It was situations like these the witch was best at solving; a little magic went a long way if a person knew how to use it. Magic is not something to be misused but sometimes Isra was okay with that. She liked being powerful, dark, and hidden. Isra enjoyed coming out of her fortress only at night, rejoicing her hatred through the dark misty skies.

She loved opening and closing mystical doors, as well as removing things that were no longer useful. This was the life she led and her heart no longer bled, for it had been torn years previously by another's inner needs but there will be more on that later. Nevertheless, she was seen as somewhat of a dark savior to all who had come to know her.

Autumn came and went, and the snow of winter fell.

It was time for another very dark spell.

2

It was a crisp moonlit night, and snow blanketed the ground. Darkness covered the land surrounding the witch's home and as it did, the witch grew in power. She never left her dwelling except to get supplies, and almost always went out in disguise for she didn't want anyone to have knowings of her comings and goings. It was important for Isra to maintain discretion.

She wasn't ugly; Isra wasn't at all what you'd think most witches would look like. This isn't like the fairytales. Isra had no green skin or crooked nose to speak of. Neither did she have gray hair.

She was slim and tall and had a beautiful bosom that was enhanced by her tight black corset, amplifying the curves of her already tiny waist. Her clear, green emerald eyes told stories, and none of them were lies. Her hair was long; it traveled down her back in ringlets of golden white curls and all around her slight frame.

Of course, people wouldn't think she was a witch by the look of her, but then many people who laid eyes on her knew straightaway: "Don't mess with her. Don't get on her bad side; she is strong, evil, and powerful." No man or animal had ever spoken or thought truer words; she was a force to be reckoned with. Isra was not someone you wanted to bump into in the middle of the night.

One cold winter's day, she ventured out in her disguise; a long black cloak and dark glasses that shielded her piercing green eyes. She was wandering around inside a herb shop in a village close to her dwelling when a being with magnificent golden wings appeared to her. Only much to Isra's unknowing and the angel's equally unaware bemusement there was a jet-black raven poking his head through the shrubbery as he watched the debacle unfold.

She thought it was an angel. She'd believed in them once, although now she had no time or care for them. The witch looked closer at the being; it was an angel indeed. The angel approached the witch and spoke.

"I did not ask to be given this job, as I do not want any part in what you do. However, I have been asked to give you a message about your calling. I am told there are many ways you can stop this destruction and dark power, but I have also been told you won't."

"Damn right she won't." Astrid marked smugly to himself. He was doing his utmost to stay out of sight. He'd been laying low for the last eleven years as he didn't want to raise eyebrows, but this was a special situation. Astrid knew firsthand how Isra felt about the love and light brigade. And she was not going to be amused by this angel's bold yet hypocritical behaviour which Astrid found even more amusing because oh golly was that angel going to get told where to go.

The witch looked up at the angel and laughed wickedly. "Well, there was a time not so long ago where I had asked you for help, and did you give it? No, you failed me, like the rest."

"You didn't ask us Isra. We were never called by you. Many forces had to step in with you after the whole calamity of your transition, but we were always on hand to help however we cannot help someone who chooses to ignore our presence." The angel stated formally.

"That's right. She never asked you for help. Not once. Oh no, she didn't need you at all." Astrid recalled with deep interest. He had been made aware the light was extremely invested in Isra way back when however she hardly paid any of it any mind.

"How can a person know help is there if you don't present

yourselves? That's the most stupidest thing I have ever heard and I've known some dimwits in my time!" Isra snapped as she folded her arms across her chest evidently getting quite annoyed with the angel.

Enraged, she continued. "No, I will not stop. I will not give my magic up. I will not surrender any power, no matter what! But on a more humorous note, I am much better than what I used to be. I have control; I can do what I want. Like you said, you never asked for this job, so go back to your army of golden messengers and leave me be."

The angel appeared shocked; the witch's response was cool, but yet also cold and calculated. "Very well. I will have to give the other the bad news, that this is your chosen path and you want nothing else. If you change your mind and want to be used for goodness, just call."

The witch scoffed and sneered. "I need you and goodness, like I need a hole in my head! Now go, and take your infernal light with you, it's blinding my eyes!"

"Oh, yikes! The ice on that comeback was just..." Astrid commented from his position perching behind the shrub but realistically now Isra was coming towards him and so he had to get out of here sharpish otherwise she might just have noticed him. And he couldn't have that.

The angel fluttered away, still shocked, but realized there was nothing that could be done to change the witch's mind. There was a time when the witch believed in angels, just like the one who appeared before her, and believed in all spiritual things and all things good and light. But alas, that time had passed. That Isra was long dead. That girl was a former memory that could never be awakened unless one dug deep enough beneath the bile and betrayal that piled on top of it.

Now it was all darkness, blood, and more darkness. Isra had no complaint about this. Isra liked things the way they were. She loved the bloodlust and torture, the darkness; she liked it, and that was just the way it was. Nobody was going to change that.

She returned to her dwelling at Shambre Fell after picking up some herbs and spices from the shop and set them about on her altar, organizing them in a triangular shape, a powerful symbol with three points. This ancient symbol represented protection.

No, she was not doing good magic, far from it, but she knew to protect herself while performing powerful, dark spells. Some energies used in spells and rituals can come back to bite you, so she was using her insurance because every witch needed a backup plan just in case a spell could backfire.

During her lifetime, Isra had cast many spells she knew to be sure to do the right things and incorporate the correct elements to avoid having problems. She was casting a spell to hide herself, to not be known, for no one to know of her existence; a powerful spell, you might say, but she had not done something of this magnitude before but yet she had an inkling of what she must do as she studied the planetary systems. The way nature behaved in midst of the elements such as rain, thunder, lightning and even the glowing serene sun. Isra understood all of it even when flowers drooped their heads nervously in anticipation of the horrors that would befall them when winter began to make its way colliding past autumn in a fiery race against time.

Isra placed her focus back to the ingredients she'd picked up from the shop. The herbs in the triangle were quickly blessed by her and then a tall, black candle was positioned in the middle. She muttered the words to the spell under her breath and watched the candle flame as it changed from a small orange yellow flame into a huge, rising black flame.

"Nicely done kiddo." Astrid motioned quietly as Isra looked pleased with her work. "Hey soon enough even the mortals won't be able to get a glimpse of you but that chicanery won't work on me. I will always be here." Astrid chuckled as he quickly disappeared beyond the iron window frame.

This was Isra's sign; it was working! She had done her bit; all would be well, and she would be hidden with only the animals noticing her.

3

I sra had always liked the idea of being invisible, and now she could be that very thing. She had often dreamed of walking the cold stone roads with no one noticing her presence. And now she could. She strolled along the forest, noticing all the glimmering dew drops in the heads of blossoming, beautiful, and mysterious flowers.

As she walked, a leaf fell upon her head, then fluttered to rest on the forest floor. She bent and picked it up. It was an orange and brown leaf with a golden edging.

She thought it was a rather special leaf, as she had never seen one like it before and felt it would go nicely on her altar. She stared at the leaf and felt it was a magical doorway just waiting to be opened.

Fairies. She had always believed in them. Powerful and mysterious beings who sometimes lived mainly in nature and normally out of sight anywhere humans were present. Isra had always wanted to meet a fairy. She once thought she had glimpsed one once but wasn't sure.

It had been a beautiful evening, and the sky was clear and the air crisp. The witch was about ten years old, and she had been playing with a childhood friend when suddenly they both saw pink lights flutter around them, dancing wildly in overblown joy to be around such playful and innocent children. They sparkled around the children with delight, and the witch always remembered how brightly colored the sparks had been, and how beautiful it was to see such a thing.

But now she was older, and that childlike innocence had vanished a long time ago. She was older than her years. While in her youth, she'd captivated the mind and heart of a child, she now thought and acted much like an old crone, even though she wasn't ancient. Barely thirty, if she cared enough to count her exact age but then again, she was immortal so it hardly mattered to her anymore. But still now, she longed to see a glimpse of that beautiful sight again for it was truly magical.

It attracted fairies to many magic, whether dark, light, from blood, or from the soul. It drew them to it like love draws souls to one to another. Interesting magnetism. Even with all her bloodlust, rage, and power, Isra was in this immensely vivid world and seeing things that no normal human being could ever see. But then again there was the whole not human thing that she had going on. Honestly fairies probably would be cautious of a witch like Isra for she had turned the tide. Exchanged goodness for dark frolics in the night and more to the point, cared very little for it. Fairies weren't keen on stuff like that.

Humans get to see the magic side of life, but they have to be attuned to it; they have to be in focus and remain open to that which governs the spirit and the soul. Then, and only then, can they be allowed to envelop themselves in all the magic and mystery the occult world offers.

Yes, she was a very dark soul, but of course, you know light cannot exist without dark. Isra used her darkness to help people, like the young woman whose husband was going to leave. It was with a blood sacrifice that Isra had saved that woman's marriage. Isra always knew when the spells worked because she would never hear from the people again.

It was good that in all her darkness, she could still help others. It gave Isra a sense of purpose. It was comforting for her soul. But that was the past, and now it was much different. Still, she longed to see these winged beings, and it would be nice, she thought, to strike up a rapport. To have a relationship with them once again.

Isra thought now would be a good time to reflect and sit back and review things, to admire her dark surroundings and allow whatever impressions came to her to be received. Quiet time and solitude.

A wonderful thing about being alone is not being bothered by anyone and being able to receive magical messages with no disturbance. It was great to walk alone in the moon- light and be surrounded by her own magical serenity; it was a time to be powerful.

Another dark spell was brewing. And this time, the witch was going to get very serious. Times were changing for now she felt a chill in the air and with that came the need for entrancing change.

4

Yet another cold winter's day and the sun had just risen; the orange and yellow rays shimmered over the little land of Shambre Fell. It was embodying the pure shimmer of light itself. Isra's dwelling was dark, but even the witch saw these rays shining through the antique glass panes and was astounded at how they had managed to sneak in. Isra went outside to investigate the light that had invaded her dark fortress for it was bemusing to her as to how such a thing could be possible.

Is it the angelics? Are they playing their trickery again? Oh, it's so garish one cannot bear the thought of it. Isra grimaced as she walked outside in the grounds of Shambre Fell.

Isra wondered at first if perhaps the angels were behind this, but then she put that thought aside and continued staring into the shimmering shades of the sun. She was planning on a different type of magic today; she wanted to merge herself with parts of a living creature, the dragon, in order to master the power of flight and pure intuition, such as transportation at the speed of light and self-healing.

The dragons were a favored creature among Isra and she rather admired them. She'd met them once before of course but that memory had faded from the carcass of her mind. Now today she was going to become like one; she wanted to maximize her strength, power, and potential, and this was the way she had set out to do it. Transformation was something she wanted to do, something she'd had in mind for a long time. It was the ultimate conduit in relation to magics. Ones she had longed to possess for such a considerable period of time that it didn't seem worth it to wait to have that any longer.

Dark magic was the only way to do it. But like most dark magic, terrible things happen. Death and gruesome sights are inevitable parts of life. Isra knew this and accepted it. Suffice to say it didn't bother her.

It grew to be late in the afternoon, and Isra began preparing herself for the spell. It would require her to be totally in tune with all that was around her, completely serene and at one with the natural world. She meditated in the forest and began chanting, continuously breathing heavy as she maintained her focus. It took some time before Isra noticed in her deep concentration that the dimly lit grassland area around began to turn a bright shade of green.

The entire forest was turning the same shade of emerald green, and after a few moments, a green dragon appeared. Isra gasped at the beautiful being that stood before her.

"Oh fuck." Astrid murmured. He'd been hiding in a nearby pine tree just wondering what Isra might be getting up to. And while it wasn't terribly stealthy of him it was the best he could do when you noted how wide open the forest terrain was. There wasn't many places for the raven to hide himself out here.

"She's only gone and summoned a bloody dragon. Oh, I do hope this is not what I think it is." Astrid commented as he watched the tall green dragon emerge right in front of Isra.

The dragon towered over her and looked straight at her before speaking. "I am all you seek; you may do with me as you please. I am here to serve you and be your divine guardian in your path of darkness. I will be your loyal servant and give you my strength and power."

"Oh, you'll give her power alright." Astrid commented as he realized what was about to commence.

Within moments, the witch took hold of the dragon's claw and admired its beauty. She paused for a minute, then revealed a dagger, pulling it from behind her back.

"Yes. Like I didn't see that coming. Taking a dragon's power well I mean it is original. I'll give her that, but does she have to be quite so graphic about it?" Astrid muttered away to himself as he couldn't tear his eyes away from Isra despite knowing what she was about to do.

Can you maybe, ahem, not do that? I mean girl I know times have been rough for the both of us but taking the life of a dragon. Surely there are better ways??? No, evidently not. Astrid chorused to himself in thought as he realized Isra was deadset on it judging by the piercing look of her.

Isra looked up at the dragon and said, "Well, my friend, I am very grateful for the gifts you'll bestow upon me. You will now be rewarded, my loyal savior."

She reached for the dragon, being careful to conceal the dagger she held discreetly in her dominant hand before she proceeded to stab him in his pure heart because there was no other way to conduct this atrocity.

"Oh jeez." Astrid turned his head away finally as it had become too much for him. He wasn't typically squeamish but this one really did irk him.

As for the dragon, he was near his besodden end. Green blood flowed into Isra and she herself emerged green as it did. It poured all over the forest floor and Isra. In fact, she was turning more and more green as the dragon slowly fell to his gruesome, bloody death. Isra stood by his corpse, staring silently before turning to walk away.

Isra had done all she'd wanted to; she had achieved this impressive feat, and now the world was hers. She had become one with the forest and now felt calmer, stronger, and more clear headed than she had been in days. This was a great day, and now, through transformation, it was going to be an even better one.

Greatness and divine power of nature and source, it was hers for the taking. Dragons were a substantial source of power and strength, and the witch had that penetrated into her. She could do just about anything she wanted to, and anything she could accomplish, she could do without fear of obstacles getting in the way.

I guess you could feel sorry for the dragon, but he was just one piece in the grand scheme of things. There were to be many more beings sacrificed and killed as time went on, and the same would go for any obstacles in the wicked witch's way. Sadly whilst her heart was absent of love, there was to be no reprieve for Isra's wickedness. It long continue until she would find reasoning to not act in such an extreme manner.

In his mind, the dragon must have known what was going to happen. Dragons are powerful and knowledgeable creatures. Obstacles only get in the way if you let them. Of course, the witch knew this and used it. She was good at that, using all her knowledge to achieve the best possible result, no matter how dangerous that result may be.

If you know nothing, how are you to succeed at anything? You must know in order to succeed, or you will surely fail because of knowing nothing. And to know something, you must study and learn, and that was something she did wonderfully, too.

Remember, knowledge is power! And power, my friend, is everything.

5

About a week had passed since Isra had killed the dragon, and the blood still stained her hands. She remembered what a beautiful bright emerald green everything had been, and how it had slowly turned her green during the transformation, entrancing her. Afterward, she'd returned to her normal color, although there were still some noticeable changes that seemed permanent long after the transformation.

Her long, fair hair had become black, and the curls were more prominent than ever before. Her eyes glowed a shade of bewitching emerald green; it was as if you could see the dragon she'd slain staring back through her eyes. The power within her was visible, and it was changing her. However, it would be unfair to say whether it was for the worse or if she was becoming better.

Slowly, day by day, Isra became darker and more mysterious. Her dwelling had changed as well, into a black color; it wasn't very colorful before having been this resounding shade of gray but now everything was black. The spell from the dragon alone had done this, and every– thing around her would soon be the same shade of black. She had been totally transformed.

The question was: what was actually left of her?

You see, Isra was slowly and surely turning into all she had done. She was becoming the very thing she'd created. It didn't look like there would ever be a way back into the good, but Isra didn't seem to mind that too much.

She had no desire to change, ever. She was a force to be reckoned with, and people were afraid of her, but they also respected her by moving out of her way when she came across the local villagers. No one dared to challenge her.

People would say, "Stay away from Isra, that vile creature who lives in the dark and hides from the light," and, "Oh my goodness, don't get on the bad side of her, for she is indeed villainous and reeks of evil."

No one dared come near her unless they needed help from her magical powers. And those that went to her did so out of dire need and desire that only Isra could help fulfill. But now, of course, no human being could see her, as she had completely hidden herself from human view.

Only animals could view the enchanting and mysterious blackened darkness that laid within. And that was just how she liked it. She had no time or care for humans, but yet admired and respected the animals, and maybe even loved the animal kingdom. Now she could go about her day-to-day business without being seen by a single living soul, and that was exactly just what she was going to do.

She was walking along a straight, narrow path. As the snow fell, she wondered what all this would lead to, and if she would ever do anything but this.

Yes, she was a creature of great power, but she was also full of sorrow and regret for things she hadn't yet done and could not have put right in her life before this time in which she lived now.

Isra had once been good, kind, and loved all, but alas, that was before.

Now she was reflecting on everything she had done in her life.

She had never been one to have many friends; many had betrayed her and not been there for her, so she learned to cope on her own. Being forced out on her own was what actually led to the darkness inside, although it was already there just lying in wait for her. Readying Isra into its undignified trap.

It was this self-reliance that led to it coming full center as she'd had enough of the torrid antics of her friends and loved ones and it had become clear then who and what she was and that this was the path she was going to walk on for the rest of her life. It wasn't the best path she could have embarked on in life, but it was the only one she had.

Isra was alone and at times; she was bitter. Isra often relished the bloodshed, torture, and lust to escape her pain from all the things she had never gotten out of life. She continued thinking of all the things from her past, reflecting on them as she walked along the cold, snow fallen path. *Just what is one to do when even love turns it's head away from you? It's not something you ever come back from is it? Once your heart is torn and shattered that is it. There is no more to discuss. It's all gone for eternity. And I will have forever to think about it.*

Suddenly, Isra saw a wriggly shape forming on the forest floor and then there were two!

As she looked closer, she noticed they were two snakes entwined in each other, totally connected. She admired the sight for a moment and then carried on walking. The animal kingdom produced and created such wonderful, prominent signs. She thought it was an omen, a connection; a strong bond that no one could break.

Lovely, she thought to herself while continuing on her journey. She wasn't headed anywhere in particular on that day; she just loved going out and about and admiring nature's wonderful sights for there was no better pursuit for her.

Isra walked a little further into a clearing by the forest. Thinking she was alone, she sat down and began meditating, concentrating on projecting her energies into the earth. She took more focus, and after a few seconds, the entire forest was black. But it was only in her vision, for when she opened her eyes, it was green and luscious and full of earthy tones again.

She heard rustling in the trees and realized she was not alone. She turned to see who or what the intruder was, and there was a magnificent green python coiled around the branches of an enormous oak tree, staring at Isra. It was clear he knew what she was and could see every inch of her being.

6

He lowered his head toward her, and she looked at him, staring inquisitively, wondering why he had noticed her and what he wanted. She wasn't used to strangers behaving like this or studying her as magnificently as he was doing.

He looked at her more deeply and spoke. "I see you at last, Lady Isra of the Dark! What an honor!"

She replied, "Why, thank you, but not all say such nice things as you, friend."

The snake smiled at her. "Yes, I can understand why. You are a dragon killer. Many here in the forest fear you, and for that, I cannot blame them at all. However, they simply do not understand a mighty creature such as you! You have amazing abilities, and you use them as you see fit; not everyone is going to accept that, but you are a very talented young lady and a magical soul."

Isra smiled at him and looked at his glowing green eyes; they reminded her of the dragon she had killed, and how she'd stabbed him in his heart and let the dragon's blood flow through her and enter her soul.

"Apparently, it's not just me watching her!" Astrid commented from the safe distance where he was situated in behind the magnificent oak tree. He'd been keeping an eye on Isra for a little while but again was keeping himself out of sight.

"You are not afraid of me?" Isra asked the python with an inquisitive glance.

"No, I am not, but I know what you are capable of, and I admire you. I hope you will kill none of my kind, for we serpents are very few, and we hope you will respect us and not encourage our number to dwindle even further. It would grieve me greatly if more of us were to perish!" He looked seriously at Isra, staring right into her bewitching green eyes. "We want you, Lady Isra of the Dark, to know that we are friend and not foe."

Isra looked at him again; he must have been over ten feet. "Very well, my friend. I give you my word that no member of the snake kingdom will come to any harm and I will respect your species and accept your offer of friendship."

The snake spoke again. "You know, there are some human beings who can still see you? You are not completely hidden, as you think. There is a human with dishonest intentions that wants you, but I do not know what for, my lady."

"I haven't caught any human males peeking their eyeballs at my witch. If they did, that would be the last thing they'd ever see." Astrid remarked in an astringent tone. He wasn't overly keen on the idea that someone could indeed be keeping watch on Isra. Of course, Astrid was exempt in this since his intention were good but still Isra had no idea who Astrid was and wouldn't do until a time came whereby Astrid felt it was safe for him to return to her.

Isra was shocked by the revelation and gasped. Her breath caught in her throat for a moment. Finally, she said, "Someone can still see me?"

The snake lowered his head even closer to her. "Yes, my lady, but this young man is going to reveal himself to you, and you will see his intentions soon enough. But for now, do as you always do and keep your wits about you. I must go but whenever you need me you can find me here in this tree. For always and for all eternity. Good day, Lady Isra of the Dark."

"Good day, my green spirited serpent."

So how come our slithery friend here knows about this fellow and not me? Perhaps I need to listen to the whispers in the trees because if someone wants to seek out Isra you can bet your life I am going to find him. Astrid discussed carefully in his thoughts. He was a little thrown by this revelation since it now meant that Isra's spell wasn't as successful as she'd deemed it to be.

Isra turned away and headed home to Shambre Fell, as she had more spells in mind after the encounter with her new green skinned friend. She liked this; after all she had no friends and had not done so for such a long time, but it was lovely to have met a guide who not only respected her but also admired her. It gave her a sense of power she could not properly describe. Isra was in awe!

Still, the main piece of information that had her curiosity flowing in all directions was the news that not only was a human being able to see her after she'd cloaked herself from the human eye, but that the mysterious man wanted something with her, either some business or maybe something else.

It was very mysterious, and she was curious, as no human in their right mind would go near her except the rare few who came to her for help. Why was this man so interested in her? Wasn't he afraid of her?

He should be, she thought to herself.

She had done the spell right, so there were no mistakes but she thought maybe he had something special about him if he possessed the ability to see her.

She cackled wickedly, then smiled at her next thought. *Well, if he has something special, neither him nor it will be around for very long!*

She did not know who he was or what he wanted with her, but she did not trust it or like it one bit. What if he was going to expose her or try to get something out of her he couldn't have? It sounded suspicious to her either way.

No one else in the human world could see her, so this man must have something they did not; maybe abilities or a hidden agenda was a possibility as well, but she did not yet know, and it was bugging her.

She had some information to go on courtesy of her new friend

Romeo, but it was puzzling her and was also stimulating her curiosity, and that was not always a good thing. But Isra was already ahead, as she now knew this was all to come and she would soon meet this mysterious man whoever he was.

Isra planned to find out his intentions, and if they were to harm her, she would kill him on the spot before he could reveal anything to other human beings about her or his encounter with her. This mysterious man had a death wish, and if he had any sense, he would drop this whole thing now.

Humans are obsessively curious to the point they cannot let something go, and that is their downfall, she thought while opening the door to her tower.

Because everything had turned black, the wooden door was now black, too. Poisoned ivy had grown through the wood of the door and sported nasty black specks on its leaves. She opened the door and walked up the long spiral staircase, while carefully noticing every step as she climbed to the top.

She had great plans, very great plans indeed! Plans of death, destruction, and bloodlust. Yes, there was a lot to do, and she had to prepare.

Isra awoke early the next morning and meditated as usual before deciding what the best course of action would be to take over the young man who was going to be in her presence soon. Would she be courteous and invite him over for a friendly chat over a nice hot cup of tea, or would she be more direct and just kill him in the middle of the forest if she didn't like what he had to say? It was worth noting Isra didn't want to cause harm to another but this man's intentions smelled less than pure so on this occasion she found herself willing to make an exception.

She had to plan this carefully because if something went wrong, it might cause her a lot of trouble. She had to plan everything down to the last detail, because, in her eyes, everything had to be perfectly planned and orchestrated right until the end.

7

———

After an hour of meditating and perfecting herself for the day, Isra concluded that the young man would come to her; she didn't need to do anything but wait and lay her trap. Isra thought of enlisting her new serpent friend but then thought better of it; he was attuned to the light and good of the world, although he also had an interest and delight in the dark which made him even more peculiar to Isra since humans shied away from the darker sides of life.

Isra would take due care to do this alone. She was going to make sure there was no intervention from the outside world; she was going to deal with it in her own unique way. This young man had better be prepared! Isra was going to be unstoppable.

She took a walk in the forest as usual and admire the scenery. The plants, the trees all bearing tempting and delicious fruits and offerings to give upon whoever picked them and rejoiced in their glorious gift, yes Isra loved it all.

The rivers and streams shone with serene aqua beauty and were calm and at peace, slowly flowing, connecting one end of life with another while washing another part of life away. The flowers' beautiful perfume and petals complimented each other in the morning sunlight perfectly in this small hour of day.

Everything was quiet, but yet the atmosphere had a somewhat changing and moving tone to it. It was early December and snow had been coming and going, not really settling but just enough to let it be known it was there, and full winter was on its way.

She slowly made her way through the forest to the tree where she'd first met her snake friend; she began tapping on its trunk with her hand and looked up to see if there was any movement. A moment later, the long green python slithered his way down and coiled himself around a branch. It delighted him to see his friend again.

"Good morning, Lady Isra of the Dark. Nice to see you again! And although this is a pleasurable surprise, I wish to know what brings you here, my lady?"

"Good morning to you... um... oh, my goodness! I do not know what to call you. Do you have a name?" asked Isra, gazing into his green eyes.

He uncoiled himself from his branch and lowered his head toward her, regarding her inquiry. "I do not have a name, for they killed my parents before I hatched."

"My goodness, that is awful. I am sorry to hear that. But you should have a name. May I name you?"

He gleamed with a smile that lit up the entire forest; he was overjoyed at the wonderful prospect Isra had brought up. "My lady, it would be a great honor if you so choose to name me. Your name brings a great fear and power to the forest, but I know in your heart that it does not come connected to the love you have for the animal kingdom, even though you seem to have forgotten that for yourself. I would love it very much if you gave me a name."

Isra sat down by the trunk and admired the roots of the tree for a moment while continuing to gaze at her friend. He was a traditional and yet loving sort, and she thought he needed something that showed pride and how wonderful he was.

"I've got it! I shall name you Romeo because of your great loving spirit and your sense of the way things are, and of course, because you are an ancient soul."

Romeo admired her for a moment and beamed again. "Romeo. I do like it a lot. Yes, I accept your wonderful offering that you have bestowed upon me. Thank you very much, Lady Isra of the Dark. Now, what brings you here?"

Isra looked up at Romeo with a second glance and then spoke. "I wish to know more of who and what this man is, and how he can see me. What does he want with me?"

Romeo closed his eyes as if to concentrate, to focus and envision what he needed to come to him while he remained in the serene thoughtfulness of the moment.

"I do not know all the answers. However, I feel this young man will come to you and reveal his intentions. It is up to you to decide what to do from there, although I feel some part of you has already decided. Again, that is your wish, just be aware that the path can change at any moment, and we always have another chance to make a change. I know you may not understand this, but you are being given a choice."

"A choice. How interesting. Yes, I have partly decided on what I will do. This young man wants something from me, but he will not be getting it. Thank you once again for your kindness and guidance."

"Well, the choice is yours and yours alone. Good day, Lady Isra of the Dark. I must get going. I have many things to do," Romeo said.

Suddenly he stopped, as he saw the inside of her heart for a moment. It was black, blacker than anything he had ever seen.

He was not afraid but wanted to step away from the moment as much as he could, for his friend Lady Isra of the Dark was going further and further down the path of darkness. He wanted a bit of light for her, although it was probably never going to happen as such creatures rarely get the chance to return to their former selves before they had become tainted.

"Well, anyway, I bid you good day and good luck, Lady Isra, and please do pop in and come again soon. You are always welcome among the serpents."

"Good day, Romeo, and I am sure we will meet again soon." Isra waved at her friend before heading off into the distance.

Maybe she could be given a last reprieve to be in the light again; he thought as he watched her shadow disappear out of the forest.

Isra continued the rest of her day after she returned to her tower, planning and in deep thought of all the things ahead. Romeo had said the man would come to her and reveal himself, so she didn't need to seek him out. Everything was more or less set in motion, but she still wanted to be ready for when that time came.

He would come and lay himself right in her trap. She wouldn't even have to lure him in; she was sure he would follow her and establish where she was. He wanted something from her (which was still unknown), but that gave her power.

The thing with Isra was, she liked power; she liked the fact they feared her and that people trembled in her very presence. It gave her an edge. A remarkable prowess that most only dared to dream about. So as to why this young fellow was seeking her out she had no comprehension of however she was quick to presume that he might be quite mad for such an idea was absurd.

Oh, what fun she was going to have with him. She would wait; she could wait. For everyone knows the best things come to those who wait.

Curiosity killed the human; she thought as she laughed to herself.

8

———————

Isra had no time nor care for humanity, and she often saw them as blistering, pus infected boils that needed removing with sharp and strong force. No, she wasn't a "people person," that was for sure. She had been embroiled in the dark ways for far too long. This was the way it was, and if she had anything to do with it, it was going to be the way it stayed, too!

Isra, Lady of the Dark, had once been human, but the very recollection of the fact repulsed her. The species disgusted her and found them revolting.

They would carry on in their merry old ways, being kind and graceful, oh, how she hated the thought of it. Why were humans so weak, refusing to look at the surrounding possibilities? They failed to see what was right in front of them.

Yes, she had a genuine hatred for them. And she would soon have an even stronger hatred for this young man, whoever he was. Because he could see her, she had already established in her mind that he might have some kind of special powers, for some humans are born incredibly gifted and attuned to the spiritual realm and magical forces of this world.

Isra's powers were dark in nature and that was one being he

should not have an interest in. But indeed, he did, and that was to be his greatest fault. Humans born with the psychic gift could often predict the future. They could even see visions and events before they happened and they had a most unusual sixth sense, very different from normal humans because they could simply sense and feel things others could not. Empathic was one way of explaining it, a gift so strong they could feel the feelings of another and be overwhelmed by them.

How disgusting, thought Isra, *to feel a million other feelings that do not belong to you.*

It all disgusted her and grimaced at the pure thought of any loving, good feeling. Whoever he was, he was laying way to his own doom because she did not have any caring feelings of love at all, and anyone who expressed them in front of her, well, good luck to them because they would surely need it.

She wondered what he looked like. She knew humans to be of a strange looking sort, with powerful personalities and facial features. He might be tall, strong, short, or weak. She paused for a moment, then figured the last thing he must surely be weak, for if he could see her, he must have some kind of power and soon she would find out what it was.

Yes, she longed to find out the reason he could see her and what he wanted with her because no man of any sort had wanted anything from Isra, Lady of the Dark, for a very long, long time indeed.

She was feeling restless that night, more restless than usual, and took a midnight stroll into the forest. It was normal for her to be awake at this time of night as she loved the night, but tonight she was feeling something. It was stirring around her, telling her something significant would happen. She locked her tower door as usual and put the key in the pocket of her long, black gown.

With her black curls flowing carelessly behind her, she made her way into the deep forest. It was dark and dimly lit; there was a tiny glow coming from the moonlight, and that was the only light that emitted through the unbroken forest, although the trees were brushing past each other's branches with the wind and everything seemed silent.

Isra paused and listened to the wind for a few moments. Suddenly, a vision came to her, and she saw a green glimmer in the corner of her eye, a glimmer of light slowly making its way over and engulfing her. Beyond the light was a shadow, a strong shadow in the shape of a figure.

Isra could see its hands, legs, and head, and it held a sword in its shadowy hand. She could see it very clearly, but the image faded after a moment and as it did, so did the green glimmer. She opened her eyes and considered it for a moment, trying to work out what it was they had delivered her.

Was it a prophecy? Showing her the very man who desired something from her so very much? Was she being given a glimpse of him to know him when she saw him for the very first time? So much pulsated in her mind, so many details and images and words flowed from her very being.

She was indeed very inquisitive and now she was being given details, so she knew it would not be long before this mysterious man would make his appearance. She wandered in the forest a little longer, touching the trees and feeling them as she went about on her way, feeling their brilliance with her soul and nourishing it as she walked, feeling ever so close to the wondrous nature and all it offered.

As she came to a clearing before the entrance to the forest, she listened closely as she heard footsteps. Isra was being followed by a shadow in the dark!

9

"Uh oh." Astrid sounded the alarm as he too was on high alert over the strong potential that Isra was suddenly not alone. He was concerned for her welfare having overheard the discussions between Isra and Romeo; her endearing snake friend, that all was not entirely clear on why this man wanted to find Isra.

Surely, he'd have better sense than that? To seek out someone regarded as wretched and unholy. But humans have this desire to control every damn thing in their shameful lives. It doesn't work well for them however but still they try! Astrid murmured to himself.

He kept his fine eyeballs on the situation. As Isra approached her blackened tower door while still listening and looking at everything around her, she reached inside her pocket for the key and slowly unlocked the heavy wooden door and left it ajar as she went inside. She climbed the long, winding staircase and continued up to her main door which led to her dwelling. Meanwhile Astrid had swerved around to the front of the tower perching himself right on the centre of the living room window sill. He wanted to ensure all was clear before he flew off. His worries for Isra were floating around in his mind. Astrid didn't like any of this. Not one bit.

Isra listened again, for she had heard more footsteps and they became closer and more easy to hear. She climbed up to the very top and slowly unlocked her main door. Pausing quietly for a moment, she arched her back and leaned against the wall as she heard the intruder enter the room. Then she flew across and slammed the door shut and locked it, keeping the key in her possession.

She turned around to face the intruder, smiling wickedly. "Bet you were not expecting that, were you my dear?"

Her intruder was a young man, aged about twenty-one with luscious blond hair. He was dressed in short jacket and leather trousers and looked at her in sheer disbelief.

"I did not think anyone was home when I entered," he announced.

"Liar, you knew I was here before you set foot in the place!" Isra screeched at him furiously. Being lied to absolutely grated on the core of her being. She detested it.

"That is indeed true, but I am looking for Lady Isra who is believed to live here. Is that you?" he asked, looking at her and trembling at the same time.

Isra moved closer to him and looked him dead in the eye. "Yes, that is me. Why do you seek me?" She asked with venom practically emitting from her lips.

The young man looked terrified; she was frightening, and she had an unnatural green shimmer in her eye that glowed menacingly every time he got close to her.

"I hear you can do many great things with magic, but older, darker magic that nobody uses anymore. I also heard you dislike humans, and I am going to be honest, you are quite intimidating, my lady!"

Isra smiled. "Intimidating I am, but you came here to my very tower. I must warn you; I dislike your kind. To be frank, humans disgust me, but you seek me for my magic, which I suspected, so you have one last chance to tell me the truth about why you are here and why you seek me. If you are here for something else, there will be no reprieve and no return to the earthly world for you. Do we understand each other?" Isra warned him, still angered by his snide manner of attempting to wheedle his way in.

The young man, still terrified, gazed at her and sincerely smiled. "Lady Isra, I wish you no harm, and I do not wish to deceive you. I promise you, I only wish to use your magic to make women love me, and that is all. For no matter how hard I try, I cannot seem to find a woman who will fall at my feet and do what I want, whenever I want. Most of them do not even want to have sex with me. I feel unsatisfied and bored." He explained to her with a wink.

It was becoming clear; he was one of those godforsaken male humans who thought purely with their penis and nothing else. He had the nerve to ask her for help in turning his situation around? Oh, she could use this to her advantage. She could teach him a lesson and make him pay, yes, she could. He wanted her magic to make women have sex with him. It disgusted her even more so now.

She knew she did not like humans and this man, a vision of selfishness, vanity, and deceit, was a good, sound reason she upheld that belief. Humans that purely thought about their own desires and gains and considered no one else in the equation. Yeah, that was another thing she could not stand about the human race; they were so selfish. *Eurgh despicable. How can one even admit to such a thing and be so confident about it? There is NOTHING to be proud about with this one. Why on earth do men like this manage to climb up the ladder of frivolity every single time? It mystifies me.* Isra commented in annoyed thought as she reviewed the situation carefully inside her mind. He had sought her out. Her. Lady Isra of the Dark. The one everyone else was afraid of. But oh no, not him. This man had been bolder than his manhood itself in coming after her in this unsolicited manner. Well, he was about to get far more than he bargained for, that was for certain.

Isra looked at him and was very serene, and calm as she spoke. "Well, that is fine, but unfortunately, I have a very strict policy here, and I am afraid I cannot help you. You wish to make things happen for your own gains. Now let me tell you how things are going to work. You are now locked in this tower; I am the only one with the key and the only way of getting out is by getting past me!" She decided quickly. *He's not getting what he came for. But we play a little game while I decide what I am going to do with him.*

He looked surprised. "Locked in your tower? Why? I have done nothing wrong. What is going to happen to me?" The young man beseeched in sheer horror of the fate that was soon to be his.

"I am a fair witch, so I will give you a chance to escape out of here and if you do not escape, then we have two very fun choices: I can either kill you, or you can become my slave. For extra fairness, I will give you a thirty second head start, although this tower is pretty complex and there is not much chance of you finding a way out," she said wickedly.

The young man trembled and looked at her in shock and horror and didn't speak for a moment as he was considering the choices: die or become a witch's slave and a nasty evil witch at that. He didn't know what option was worse.

He did not want to die, but, he did not want to be her slave either, because he did not know what he was going to be made to do. Not only that, he did not know if she was telling the truth and was going to keep to her word, for he feared she may just decide to kill him, anyway.

He wasn't wrong; Isra had no intention of sparing him or letting him get out of this easily. Isra wanted to study the young fellow so that in the meantime she might discover just how he had been able to see her in the first place. But she also enjoyed games, so the escape idea was going to be played out first.

The young man, still terrified, looked at her and spoke. "So, I am to be killed or become your slave? May I ask why I cannot just get my spell and leave?"

She laughed coldly, for she had expected this response and was prepared for it. He seemed to think he could have all life offered him handed to him on a silver platter. He thought everything was going to go his way and now she was showing him that this would not be the case this time.

Hahaha. Oh, it just gets better and better doesn't. Get your spell and leave? Do I look like I was born yesterday? Hell no. You came here for a reason and I will be damned if I am letting you loose into the world after knowing such darned intentions lie deep inside your soul. No, we'll play this my way and then we will see what shall become of you. Isra muttered solemnly in her thoughts. She was feeling very calculating and as menacing as she was, Isra wasn't sure if she was going to dispose of him just yet. Like all things, it would come to her in time.

"I may have mentioned to you I do not like humans. I simply cannot let you leave this tower; you may try to escape, but like I said, that is very hard. I have locked every door, and there are windows, but they are not big enough for you to squeeze through. It's very simple: play my game, and you either lose or you win."

"So, I cannot get my spell. Is that what you are saying? And you offer a proposal which you know will benefit you either way? My goodness, Lady Isra, you really are wicked, your soul is rotten to the core!"

"Yes, I am, but you stalked me, followed me into my home, and now you are in this tower. You can't leave it. Rules are rules, I am afraid, and as for your spell, you are not worthy of it. You are not worthy of something like that. The only thing you deserve is to be punished, and I have a pretty good way to start," she laughed.

"Well, since there is going to be no way out, I guess I have no choice but to accept your offer of becoming your slave. I only ask that you reconsider your thoughts about me deserving punishment because I do not. I only wanted women to love me and to do everything I please as a way of experiencing that emotion. I guess that falls on deaf ears with you, my lady."

"I guess you fucked up there, buddy." Astrid remarked with a tang of amusement before he proceeded to shove off. Isra had the situation handled. She was in no immediate danger. He could catch some juicy worms and reconvene to check on her tomorrow.

"No, you did not. You wanted to control them. Now you are being punished; remove your shoes, as slaves do not need shoes."

He did as he was told and removed his black leather boots. He was helpless, with no weapons and barefoot in the witch's tower; would there be any escape for him?

Who knows, but he was pretty much doomed at this point.

10

I sra ordered him to clean and sweep her basement, so he was well occupied. She hadn't bothered to ask what his name was. Isra did not care. She had a new slave and was protecting innocent young women as a further result. She was pleased with herself and wondered what extraordinary things would delight her today.

Isra had decided she would go to see Romeo to update him on the news of the man and what had happened with it all. He would be glad to see her, for the witch had not talked to anyone as much as she did Romeo. She left the boy with instructions on what to do and locked the main door, venturing out into the clearing, slowly disappearing into the forest.

Isra walked for quite a while when she came to a stream she had not come across before and knelt beside it so she could put her hand in the water and bring it to her face. It was cool and cleansing; she felt good. She thought she would sit here for a while and ponder things; she enjoyed pondering, putting all the deep thoughts together and organizing them in her head until they made sense and were all sorted into their separate boxes.

Well, she called them "thought boxes," but basically, she sorted the good thoughts and kept them in one part of her brain, and the bad thoughts were discarded. Of course, with Isra, the good thoughts were indeed the nasty, devious, and dark thoughts, and the bad ones were all the things she did not love, like humanity and caring. She binned those right away, for she had no use for them.

After an hour of sitting by the stream and ordering her thoughts into their rightful places, she walked a different way home. She came across a path that she had never found before and walked into a dark, deserted valley. There was nothing living here, very little trees and no grassy banks or meadows.

The desert was fiery and dank. It had nothing to show for it, no plants or trees, no water to be seen anywhere and there was a distinct eerie feel to this place that disturbed the witch slightly. Isra wasn't afraid, but she knew by the chill in the air that something was definitely not right with this place.

There were clearly no animals of any kind there, and she could see spots where fire pits had once been. It was a place of sheer danger. She walked a little further and stopped for a moment because she heard rustling coming from the shrubbery that was situated alongside the clearing.

Isra could not work out what it was or where it was coming from, but it was clear it was not very far away from her, and whatever it was, she was the target. She stood completely still and listened to the air around her and retreated slightly, only to fall into a giant pit, plunging into darkness. Isra gasped, "Oh my." As she felt herself lose her grip on gravity. The fall was high, but she was not injured.

She dusted herself off quickly, only to find herself in a pit full of snakes, their eyes all staring back at her as she stood watching them. They surveyed her carefully, hissed loudly, and made their attack.

Isra assessed this was a rapid developing situation so she immediately stood on one long winding snake and grabbed another as she shouted out.

"SILENCE! What is this?!"

The snake in her hand gulped, and the rest stopped their attack.

She was close to strangling the one in her hand, and the one on the floor beneath her feet was almost suffocating underneath her feet.

A hundred eyes were all on her at that very moment before one, an older green and yellow snake, spoke. "My dear lady, we are sorry, but orders are orders. A man called upon us and said that you should be destroyed immediately, for he said you are a menace to society, and therefore must be stopped."

She straightened herself up and said, "Is that right? Who said this, exactly?"

The green and yellow snake spoke again. "He is a warrior of this land and has some power, but not much. A bit of a dabbler, you might say, but he has a habit of making things happen. And as for his description, he is young, about twenty years old, with golden blond hair. He wears unusual clothing: black leather boots and a jacket. He insisted we get rid of you immediately."

Isra laughed for the first time since falling in the pit and smiled while eyeballing the snakes. "I will have you know that a young man matching your description is locked in my tower right now for crimes of deceit and deception over the human world. He cannot get messages to anyone. Now tell me, do any of you know a python named Romeo?"

The snake looked up at her and smiled. "Yes, he is our leader. Why do you ask?"

Isra laughed. "He and I are great friends. I even named him."

The green and yellow snake bowed apologetically. "My lady, I am so sorry. I did not know you were close friends with Romeo. You will come to no harm here, and I am sorry about the confusion with the young man, but he sent us a message that you were to be destroyed. I give you my word that will not be the case here."

Isra let the snake go, and the others parted in front of her. "It doesn't matter; I will deal with him. He is already a fool for encountering me, but now he is an even bigger fool for attempting to rid the world of me. I leave you all be and thank you for your kindness, but this man will soon be no more. Tell me how one gets out of this pit?" Isra quizzed the elder snake with a look of concern.

She'd fallen down here and yes it was swift but now came the challenge of lifting herself back up to the surface.

"Oh, if you hold onto to those rocks on the side wall, you should be able to reach the top. I am once again sorry for the misunderstanding." The elder snake chirped in her direction. He had felt bad for making such a rash course of action under the instruction of a mortal who was clearly not invested in being a good soul.

"Thank you, dear friend." Isra mustered as she quickly lacked on to one of the rocks, hooking her left ankle over the right one as she lifted herself up from the ground.

And with that, Isra climbed from the pit, and the snakes watched as she disappeared back into the forest. She was puzzled; *how could this man send a message to the army of snakes while he was locked in her tower?*

He must have some kind of power, power that she was going to destroy, but first, she would make him suffer for this foolish act. *Yes, he must suffer*, she decided, and laughed as she strolled home.

She came up to her tower door and unlocked it carefully while quickly locking it again and slowly climbed the long spiral staircase that led to her main door to her dwelling. She paused for a moment and listened, for she heard footsteps and this meant her prisoner was actively doing something up there, most likely scrubbing floors.

Oh, how she loved it when people tried to get one over on her. She loved how stupid they looked. She was going to tell her slave about his foolish attempt, but she was going to add some fun to it first.

Isra came to him after she descended down to the basement and instructed him on a new set of tasks. "Well, my dear, it is a cold and forlorn day, so let's have all the windows washed, and the ceilings wiped, and all the floors scrubbed as punishment for your stupidity!"

The young man looked on and asked, "My stupidity?" She laughed. "Yes, your stupidity for trying to have the army of serpents come after me while I was out this morning. You foolish, imbecile, how dare you try such an act when I have been kind enough not to kill you!! It is no matter, you humans never learn unless you are punished, so you will do as I say and then I will decide on how to deal with you. Off you go!"

He seemed ashamed and looked up at her, but she looked furious. She was glowing red with fury from eye to eye, and her eyes were green as ever but now tinges of her anger were clearly visible.

"Okay, if that is what must begin, then that is what will be. I will go."

She pulled him toward her for a moment and whispered, "Yes, but you will never leave here alive; that soul of yours is rotten, and you have made a fatal mistake, boy!"

He trembled and ran to do what he was asked as she stood behind him, watching every move. He was in for it now; he had well and truly pissed off Isra, Lady of the Dark. Who knows what terrible fate was now in store or what horrible things she would bestow on him?

One thing was clear: he would not get out of this thing intact because now he'd made the serious misjudgment of attempting to relieve the universe of Lady Isra of the Dark.

11

The next day Isra rose early and took some time to bathe in the sunlight and its healing rays before making a point of checking up on her slave. She was excited in a wicked sort of way to deliver her next form of mental torture. She wanted something subtle yet poignant, something that would surely show how menacing and evil she was.

Isra wasn't best pleased he had tried to sabotage her by telling a tall tale to the army of serpents, and she wasn't one for letting grudges go easily. He would pay for his crimes to her and the world, yes, he would. She just hadn't yet decided what his punishment would be.

Isra had waited for him to arise from the cold stone floor. When he did and entered her room, she had a few things in mind for him. But Isra had decided on a different approach. She greeted him this morning with a smile and playfully tapped him on his shoulder.

"Good morning, dear sir. I hope you are well and not too uncomfortable. If you please, I wish to ask your name as I do not know it." She mustered sweetly. Something that would put any captive on edge since she hadn't done this with him before.

He looked taken aback at the witch's request, but obeyed all the same. "My name is Kane. I come from a family in the woods; they will wonder where I am."

Isra remained calm and replied, "Do not fear, that is no longer a problem for you. It is great to have met your acquaintance, Kane. Tell me, do you feel up to something a little different this morning?" She asked, again not letting on as to why her different change in tone.

Kane straightened and ran his fingers through his wavy hair and smiled; *maybe she is changing, maybe she would spare me. Perhaps my luck is about to change for the better?* Many thoughts ran through his head as he answered Lady Isra of the Dark.

"Yes, my lady, I feel I could be up to something like that. What is it?" Kane inquired with a wistful glare.

Isra turned to him, wistful and sweet, and smiled again. "Well, I know you have some kind of power. I cloaked the human living world from seeing me, and somehow you still did just that. Plus, I know you had a meeting with the snakes and tried to get me killed, but that is all forgotten now. I wanted to ask you if you could see something standing in my way for a spell I will do soon; do not worry if you cannot, but I thought I would ask." She requested, just as kind as she already had been only a moment ago so that it had sounded as though he had a choice.

"Oh boy, she has him under her thumb alright. The charming young man got far more than he bargained for in this circumstance." Astrid ventured from his sacred spot as he peeked in through the window to get a bird's eye view on what was going on. His amusement didn't go unnoticed as he let out a sly chuckle emitting, "Talk about a fall from grace. She says jump and the boy asks just how high he can climb that ridiculously tall mountain. Oh my. It's distasteful but it is quite the show to feast my eyes on."

Kane replied, "I will try to help in any way I can, but I normally have a bowl of water I used to scry. It's been a talent of mine and my family's for many years now, and we use it to predict things and events. I will try my very best for you. Thank you for allowing me to help, my lady."

He thought he was onto a good thing now. He really did, but he didn't stop for a moment to pause and think, "What the hell is she up to?" which is exactly what he should have been asking himself. Any man in their right mind in that glory forsaken moment would have done exactly that but Kane was too naive to presume that this was some tactic that Isra had plucked from her wide array of tools she had at her disposal.

Make him think he's got hope. Keep him hanging on by the sides of his guts while he's keen enough to involve himself in my dark world because then and only then will he have convinced himself that it's going to be fine. Duh. Isra mocked Kane callously in her thoughts. Sometimes it required a little bit of finesse in order to gain the upper hand on someone.

Isra fetched the bowl of water and eyed him sweetly. He was nervous. What on earth could the witch be up to? Still, he hoped his future with Lady Isra was changing for the better.

Kane sat cross legged on the floor whilst gazing at the bowl of water as Isra quietly stood behind the door listening and watching through the hinges. There was the odd presence of her being, as if he could sense her from a faraway location, and it was very clear she was there. Isra didn't want to miss anything, so she stood silently, waiting for any developments.

Kane stared at the bowl, closing his eyes for a moment to focus and concentrate on the water. At first, there was nothing, barely a few ripples which he had made with his finger by waving it around in the water for a while, but then a white flash appeared and startled him.

It reminded him of something he had seen when he was very young; angels had come to him and told him he would do great things. This flash of light was not an angel though, this was indeed something else. It felt otherworldly which was new territory for Kane since being a seer that type of stuff was not his forte.

Kane continued to stare and paused as it got brighter, right in front of his face, almost blinding him. Then it merged into a circular shape and encircled around him before disappearing into nothingness.

The water was now as clear as it was before the white light

appeared. He wondered what it was he had just seen. It made no sense why this white light would surround him.

Was it an angelic being letting him know it was there and protecting him? Kane came from a family of spiritual people who were indeed very gifted and saw things before they happened, but alas, he was now held prisoner by Lady Isra of the Dark. What was he going to tell her?

She wanted to know if he could see anything that would stand in the way of her next spell. Isra had already cloaked the human world from seeing her, but yet he still could. Was he immune to her power? He hoped and prayed that would be so instead of some weird occurrence that he simply could not comprehend.

Perhaps he would just tell her everything was fine, and he'd seen nothing. He couldn't tell her he'd seen a white protective light that had indeed surrounded him. No, he could not say that at all; he would instead say that nothing was going to stop her from casting her next spell. That was a much safer bet.

He rehearsed it in his head for a few moments before approaching her room in which she sat, doing her spells and reciting potions and words of mystery, power, and magic. But what he did not know was that Lady Isra of the Dark already knew what Kane had seen, and she suspected it was yet another angelic interference. However, she was waiting for his response before deciding what to do with him next.

She wanted to make him squirm in his uncomfortable position, make him sweat a little. She was going to get as much pleasure as she could from this young man who had made an enormous mistake when he'd encountered Lady Isra of the Dark. If only he knew how much of a mistake it truly was.

He tiptoed into her room, surveying his surroundings as he entered. In the centre of the room lay a black iron cauldron on table, and in front of it lay glass bottles containing all kinds of herbs, potions, powders, and other sorts of things. Next to the cauldron was a big, black, heavy book with ancient and tattered pages. Isra had the book open at the center, and on top of it was a black skull holding it open.

The entire room held a mysterious, and yet also deadly, atmosphere. He could smell she was planning something and yet he did not know what, but part of him also did not want to know. She was far too capable of doing something horrid to spend too long thinking of what kind of deadly deed it would be.

He straightened up and stood by her, and waited for her to look up and notice him. She had been reading the comprehensive book and was slightly startled, as she seemed deep in thought as he approached her table.

"Good afternoon, Kane. I trust everything went well? The little scrying session showed no problems or obstacles in my way?" she said sweetly, causing him to gasp a little.

"Yes, my lady, it went fine. I could see nothing that stands in your way. You are free to do whatever you wish, and it will be successful." He explained to her without delay which made her pleased judging by the expression on her face. One that unnerved Kane just a little bit more than he was showing as he stood there with gritted teeth just relishing the opportunity to get back down to his basement.

Isra was revelling, her face beaming with sheer delight. She could do what she had planned, and nothing or no one was going to stop her.

12

Kane, however, was not laughing. Her slave was now in a state of panic as he fully realized what he had gotten himself into. A mere attraction seemed worthless now compared to this, seeking a woman who could kill him with her bare hands.

What an idiot I am, he thought dryly.

Why hadn't he listened to the townspeople who warned him about Lady Isra? Why hadn't he listened to Ronald? His father? The people who knew him and cared for him the most. Surely their intentions would not have led Kane astray? But oh no, he'd wanted to see it for himself. Kane had that strong habit of always wanting to prove people wrong and now it had backfired on him because he was in way too deep.

Instead, he had gone out and sought the witch! Everyone in his village had told him of how in the forest a lady named Isra was the most powerful force on the earth; she had once been human, but was now consumed by darkness.

He had also been told that she used her powers to transform herself and take a dragon's power while becoming blackened, and everything around her also became blackened.

Kane had been told this tale and was still interested in finding the witch. He had expressed an interest, for he thought as a young male she would be useful to him if he could get his hands on her. He wanted her power. He wanted to benefit his village and also a prominent part of himself.

Oh, how foolish he had been. His own selfish and despicable greed had now led to him being locked in the witch's tower with no way of escape and no guarantee he could return safely home, and definitely no chance of getting his hands on the witch's power. He was barefoot, with no weapons and no way out of his mess.

If only he had ignored his curiosity, but there was no point dwelling on it now; what was done was done, and now he needed to focus on the here and now. He would surely need a miracle if such things existed. But what about what he had seen in the bowl of water when he was scrying?

Maybe some kind of miracle was nearby, maybe even watching over him as he lived and worked in the witch's tower, watching his every move and making sure he was safe and not yet dead. But Kane didn't really believe in miracles; he was a magical man by birth, but he did not believe in miracles.

Kane was born into a family of gifted seers, psychics, and clairvoyants. He had been raised by a stern father, a seer who believed in old fashioned values, and that a man should fight for what he believed to be true. His mother was a gypsy and more interested in the laws of nature and taking care of Mother Earth rather than fighting.

Kane had all the attributes of a born gypsy, but he was more interested in sword fighting, fencing, and defending what's right in his village despite his gifted heritage. He was a warrior at heart, but it was his driven ego that led to his selfishness and greed, the same greed and selfishness that made him seek the witch.

Kane wanted women to love him; he wanted them to be at their beck and call and for them to do whatever he pleased. He had little success on the love front, but he did what he could despite his ego that wanted nothing more than sex and power. His mistake was seeking the witch, Lady Isra, who knew deep down his intentions were not good, so she punished him for trying to hide them and for trying to use her to get what he wanted.

She did not like that kind of deceit and would not accept it from any human being, never mind a man who thought the entire world revolved around him. Especially the female population, who he wanted nothing but admiration and respect from.

He had been born a good, loyal man and was an excellent warrior at heart, but alas, yet again, his ego had gotten him into trouble. He thought of what things would be like when he got home. If he got home.

He thought to himself wistfully, *If I survive this, by God I will change my ways. I will be a better man. I will be the warrior my father wants me to be. I will be good. I will do well. But only if she doesn't kill me first.*

13

There was light in all things, and Kane truly believed in his heart that this, like all things would turn out good in the end and everything would be fine. He had a great optimistic attitude about him. No matter how many scrapes he'd gotten himself into, he always got out of them with his positive but yet also strong mind and attitude.

I will survive. I'll get out of this. I will. Peace will come and I will triumph and then it will just be an afterthought. By goodness and glory, I'll break free. I know that the end is in sight.

Kane continued these thoughts for a few moments and paused before thinking again, *Maybe there is some good in her, maybe deep down she is not so bad. She might even let me live, and I can be free to live with my family again. Perhaps I can find the good inside her somewhere under that murky exterior.*

He picked up a broom and prepared to sweep the witch's basement. He would keep himself busy with his chores today, and the basement was very dusty and had had little love or attention for a few years. Lady Isra had been complaining about the dust gathered around the place, but had neglected the housekeeping over the tenure she'd occupied the majestic chateau. So he got to work on his chores and kept in mind that there is good in all things, even a wicked creature that does not want to be loved.

Lady Isra was joyous knowing that she could do her next spell without being interrupted by the human world. She could do exactly what she wanted, and she was already planning the next idea. She had already cloaked the human world from seeing her; now she wanted to go further in her magical arts.

Isra began consulting her enormous book of spells and was perusing a few pages and holding the book open with the black skull that normally sat on top of the book when it was not in use. She came across a few she had used before, but she didn't want to use something she had already done; she wanted to be creative with this.

Isra wanted something that people would not think was her doing. Something clever. Something unknown to mortals and animals alike. She looked and searched and searched until she finally had an idea. What she had in mind was to transform herself into something, an animal or an object perhaps, to venture into the human world and gather information so she could plan more easily. She wanted to be stronger. She wanted to be better.

Isra was going to make sure she was neither seen nor heard, and every witch needs a good disguise, right? She had already killed the green dragon, but the forest (including her friend, Romeo) already knew about that, so she would not be well hidden. She would have to think of something else. This task needed a feat that Lady Isra of the Dark had never accomplished before.

14

Transformation is a powerful word, not just the word itself, but the main being inside it. To transform means to become something or someone, to change something that was not already there.

Lady Isra of the Dark would have to study very hard if she was going to come up with something that would fool the rest of the human world and hide her identity. Many knew of the witch's existence, but not all knew what she looked like and this is where she would have the upper hand because she would hide so well that she would, in fact, blend in with the rest of her surroundings.

Isra had at first thought she would change into an animal. She had a lot of respect for the animal kingdom and her most trusted and only confidant, Romeo was a serpent. Another being that symbolizes change and transformation. She would converse with Romeo before this transformation would occur for he would be sure to advise her on what was best before she proceeded with anything.

Then she thought again, and concluded she would blend in and be more cunning by changing herself into an inanimate object, something that would be still and be able to see and listen to everything around it. Or maybe something that nobody around her would even dare to suspect concealed her fine form underneath it.

The power needed for this spell would take a lot of preparation in order to gather the energies needed to transform herself into whatever she desired. Isra would need to work very hard to get it right and would have to get rid of all distractions and the number one distraction at the moment was her slave boy, Kane.

He was a remarkable human, very gifted, but had a colossal ego to match. He came from a village full of gifted people and had heard about the witch from his fellow villagers and wanted more than anything to seek her out. This was in the hope she may help him win over the women of the village with her magic, but alas, this had backfired on him and now he was locked in the tower and forced to be Isra's slave. Not one of his finest moments, was it?

Kane was scrubbing the walls as Lady Isra sat in quiet contemplation of what was to be her next move. She was going to transform herself in order to get some more information and knowledge of the outside world. The question was, what?

Lady Isra had gone and see Romeo. She had quite a connection with Romeo and felt like she had known him for a very long time. She had not been to see him for a while. She had planned to see him a few days ago but wandered off into a clearing and fell into the pit of snakes where she had discovered Kane had somehow contacted them, telling them they needed to rid themselves of her.

But today was different. Today, there would be no interference from any outside influences.

Isra had started early on her walk and made sure she was not seen. She made her way into the clearing, listening to the wind as the branches of the trees moved in the air before she then approached the tree where she'd first met Romeo and gave its trunk a knock to let her presence be known.

She listened and heard movement from the top of the tree, and looked up to see what was above. Sure enough, a green figure emerged and slowly came down the tree. Romeo saw the knocker was

Lady Isra of the Dark and greeted her with a smile before speaking to her and watched as her piercing green eyes looked back at him.

"Good morning, my lady! I trust you are well? I have not conversed with you in quite a while and do hope you are in good health." He retorted in a friendly voice.

Lady Isra looked up at her friend. "Yes, I am very well, thank you. The boy you mentioned found me. He made the mistake of following me home one day and now he is locked in my tower. I made him my slave. You were right about his intentions, my friend, and he is being punished for them now."

Romeo smiled. "Yes, I thought he would come to you. Well, you do what is best with him, Lady Isra of the Dark. Please tell me, what brought you to my neck of the forest?"

"Of course, friend, I wish to learn more about the world I am living in, I wish to learn what makes humans do the things they do and how they behave. I wasn't in their world long, and never paid much attention when I was. Now I am eager to learn." She detailed in a low voice. Isra was taking due care as to who might hear her for there was many whispers deep in this part of the forest and she was going to be as sneaky as she could possibly muster.

"I thought you might be curious about the human world soon enough. They are becoming more and more interested in you, my lady. The one you have taken is, in fact, a warrior. Well, he would be if he wasn't so greedy and deceitful to his people, including the fair maiden he was engaged to marry soon. I imagine his people are wondering where he is, but that is no problem for you, of course," he blurted out which left Isra hanging on tenterhooks.

Oh wow. He has a bride? Someone he's engaged to? Oh my. This is just..... I mean how can one be so stupid not to see what they have right in front of them? It's preposterous. My giddy heart. If it was still beating it would be on its last beat right now.... Isra collided around inside her mind as the thoughts circled in a fury. It was almost too good to be true. *But why would Romeo lie? He wouldn't.* Kane had to have this mysterious bride he was engaged to be married to floating around somewhere. The question was, where?

Romeo paused and was glad he did so. The last thing he wanted to do was upset Lady Isra of the Dark. Although he was a serpent and had his own brand of power, he had witnessed her killing the dragon and then the transformation in which she took his power and her world and almost everything in it had become blackened; he knew what she was capable of.

Romeo knew there was no goodness in her heart and if there was; it was buried under much blackened darkness that surrounded her to the core of her being. She watched with big, wide eyes as she noticed him pause, so said, "I guess this young man's mistakes are his and you shall do what is right for you, my lady. What is it you wish to learn?"

Lady Isra looked delighted. "I had no sign he was engaged. He came to me seeking a spell that would make women love him so he could control them. I wish to study them more deeply, the humans that is, so that I may gain a deeper knowledge of them and also find ways of keeping myself hidden." Isra explained coyly. She was hardly being subtle here. It was obvious she wanted to use a ploy as a deception, but the greater motive was not being revealed. That was something that made Romeo drop his head down a little lower for he didn't know what her intent was.

Romeo sighed. Lady Isra wanted to remain hidden, and this learning, he feared, was to be another surge of great power. "You wish to learn more about them and also better yourself in the process of this learning?" He asked her inquisitively.

"Yes, dear friend. I wish to be in their midst, be in the backgrounds of their mundane lives and watch them as they live and weep among one another while expressing their joy and trying to contain their sorrow." Isra made her connotation known but still not completely revealing what her desire was.

Romeo thought for a moment. Whatever advice he gave to this lady, he would have to be careful, as one wrong word could make him her next victim, no matter how much respect and friendship they shared.

What is the motive behind this? He thought. *What is she up to? Why would an already powerful witch want to see how the other half lives? What could she possibly want with the human world?*

He pondered and pondered the question, but whatever the answer, there would be no genuine or good intentions involved so it was best for him to guide her to the best of his ability because he didn't need to delve further as to where she was headed.

<h1 style="text-align:center">15</h1>

Isra, Lady of the Dark, well, her soul, to be more precise, was already rotten to the core. She needed no more power. There was enough inside her, coursing through her very being.

She had long dreamed of power and glory when she was young. She had been a spiritual being once upon a time, believe it or not, but that time had long passed. No more were the days of believing in angels, spirits, and other aspects of good and spirituality. She was a full-blown witch and she liked it that way.

Her path had not been easy. She gave up her spiritual practice and became interested in the darker matters of life and so started embracing them. First, she became interested in revenge spells, seeking revenge on those who had wronged her, and these worked great much to her satisfaction. People would come to her for help with revenge on others, but she looked for something more.

There was something about black magic that appealed to her. Control. She had always wanted to control her fellow human beings and to have power over them. Power was another one she was fond of. Binding was also a great interest to her. She loved how she could control a person and the outcome of a situation by binding that person and therefore stopping them from screwing up anything she had planned to do or what someone envisaged onto another person. It was very important to know that Isra often practiced magics that went beyond the core of darkness but were designed to help or save another soul from some kind of trickery that someone else was placing upon them.

Isra had often added blood to the casting when she did a binding spell. It was an ancient art, binding oneself to a person or their will in order to control them. It had always worked, and following the success of these spells, Lady Isra of the Dark slowly learned her craft and eventually moved to a place where few knew of her existence. She could do her work without being disturbed. It had been that way for many years now since she'd occupied the prestigious castle at Shambre Fell.

Isra had lived in her tower for years. She had acquired it easily and at low cost. The previous owner, also a witch, died because of mysterious circumstances which Lady Isra had questioned as she found it strange what she was being told. She was very young at that point, but was also thankful to have found a home in the forest where no humans were present.

Lady Isra was getting fidgety, so Romeo thought quickly and looked down at her as he answered. "The one thing humans do best is joy and sorrow. You wish to be in their midst, unseen by them? Because you will want to be hidden, won't you, my lady?" He asked her.

Lady Isra smiled. "Oh yes, of course, it's how I work best, my friend. It is also the best way I can learn, as I can just sit and observe with no knowledge of them knowing I am there." She retorted with eager enthusiasm.

Romeo leaned closer and looked into Lady Isra's eyes, gleaming as green as ever. "Then a transformation would be best, although not the same as you did with the dragon, you understand. It needs to be a little more detailed, and you won't need as much control over this one. Just manifest yourself into something that can simply sit back and watch their every move, if that is what you wish, my lady."

"Will I need much study and preparation for that?" Lady Isra asked.

"It may take a little, but not very much for you. I imagine you are already one of the wise ones and need little intuition in these matters. Especially in areas of magic, such as transformation. I watched you as you took the dragon's power and may I say, it fascinated me to see such a young lady be so in control and focused on the task at hand."

"It was quite a feat. I was in a trance for very little time before I felt the power envelop me. I remember everything around me going green. I remember it well." Isra recalled as she had found her transition very intriguing despite the lengths she had gone to get done what she had needed to.

"Yes, of course, you remember, my lady, for that was the premise that led to your blackened transformation and the source of the way you are now as you stand before me," he said quietly.

Isra was very precise and didn't miss a trick. Her eyes moved around, following whatever had her interest. It was a butterfly. Lady Isra's bewitching green eyes followed it as it brushed past the tree and went around onto a nearby flower. Her eyes could follow anything anywhere, a stolen gift from the dragon.

She was eerie in that manner; she was also very good at smelling rats, human rats who told lies. Yes, she was excellent at sniffing out those. Lady Isra noticed Romeo's long pause and stared at him inquisitively for a moment or two.

He caught her glance and quickly straightened up and looked back at her, staring at her long, flowing black curls that graced gently past her dress and down her back, effortlessly with so much elegance.

"I imagine you would remember it, my lady, for I remember it well and I was in this tree watching as you embraced the dragon, spoke to it, and then again as you stuck the dagger into his heart." Romeo retorted in a serious voice, but he was trying very hard not to upset her by being too blunt. The last thing that he wanted to do was anger her.

Isra smiled and looked at Romeo fondly. She was proud of herself and what she had done. "Yes, my friend, it was indeed a beautiful day."

The time was getting on, and Romeo wanted to get back safely to the top of his tree. He was a snake and had his own powers, but he wanted to get away from Lady Isra of the Dark as fast as possible. The way she kept looking at him and gazing into his eyes was making him very nervous, and as a snake, that was not something he was going to willfully admit.

She had something about her, something that gave her an edge. Oh, she had power. There was no question about it, and she knew how to use it. He was seeing just how much power she had and was worried about who or what it would get used on.

He slowly uncurled himself and stretched out. "Well, my lady, I must get on. I have got things to do up here. Winter is still harsh, so I must rest, too." He excused himself, eyeing up the safe spot where he dwelled at the top of the oak tree he had called home.

Lady Isra looked into the sky and saw the night slowly coming in upon them. "Yes, that is true. Winter is still very much with us, but it will be spring soon, and with spring comes change, and with change comes more of what we do not expect. Sleep well, my friend. I must be off as well; the slave boy has been on his own in the tower all day." Isra announced before she turned to walk away from him for their leisurely chat was well and truly over.

Romeo watched as Lady Isra of the Dark completely disappeared into the forest, but then she did that very well. Isra appeared and disappeared just as quickly as one and the other. She was also good at reappearing when one least expected her to which wasn't always welcomed by some.

16

Isra opened her tower door and made her way upstairs, only to find no sign of Kane anywhere. Unworried, she made herself some tea to warm up from the cold that had set in from outside. She sat as her tea brewed and smelled the richness from inside the cup, winter berries and fragrant warm cinnamon as a final touch, and let her senses be bathed in the wondrous rich flavor. She held the cup in her hands and prepared to put her lips to it.

It was very warm and refreshing as she drank. She loved natural herbal tea made from herbs and fruit. Isra had always been fond of natural remedies.

Isra all of a sudden had heard footsteps; perhaps Kane was in the basement. She had a pretty good handle on him as she had held him prisoner in her tower but she was being used to his presence in the tower.

She finished her tea and put the cup on the table. Kane would wash it later. He was reluctant at first; he was not comfortable with the arrangement, but now he had accepted it, for he had an unwavering faith that all would turn out well in the end.

Yes, he was very useful to her, but she intended on using him in other ways, too. She had already asked him to use his gifts to see if anything would stand in the way of her next spell, which he did, but had lied to her about what he saw. Isra had already decided she would do nothing about it for the moment and she was sticking to that because other things were sure to await her interest.

Isra paused for a moment before heading down to the basement. She closed the main door and went down the stairs, watching herself as she went, and then followed another set of stairs that led into the basement. Once at the bottom, she opened the door and looked inside.

At first, she did not see Kane. Isra couldn't see anything for a few minutes, as there was smoke everywhere. She wasn't sure what had been happening here, but the smoke blinded her a little, and once she waded her way through it, she saw Kane, cross legged on the floor, leaning against the wall with his head down, staring at the floor. Isra stood watching him for a moment, staring inquisitively at him.

She wondered where the smoke was coming from; perhaps he had stolen one of her incense sticks. She walked over to him until she was standing in front of him.

Her gaze fixed so intensely on him that he suddenly stopped what he was doing.

Her glowering stare was, in fact, burning him as she continued to stare and suddenly smiled.

This sort of behavior from Lady Isra worried Kane, as he truly did not know what she would do next. When a witch smiles, it cannot be for a good reason; something must happen, something wicked, something evil.

She must have something brewing inside her, he thought.

He looked up at her and grimaced in reaction to her smile; she creeped him out when she did this. She would go from nasty to nice in a few seconds, and he got freaked out each time she did so. Isra's calm exterior was too much for him, as he had not long realized just what he had got himself into by seeking the witch for her power. He had indeed been a fool.

"Hello, my lady, pleasant walk, I presume?" he said in eager anticipation of a pleasant response.

Lady Isra smiled again, this time eviler, and he grimaced even more at the sight of it. "Yes, my friend, it has been a beautiful day, a day full of power and learning, and I am soon to master the next wonderful skill that has been put in my pathway." She announced, still smiling which only put him more on edge.

He tried forcing a smile but could not. She talked about her evil with such passion. A beautiful day of learning and power was what she'd called it. Yes, that was a subtle way of saying she loved being evil and loved doing what she did best, controlling events and people, destroying things and sending her wrath and fury everywhere she went.

He feared her; he found her intimidating, but he also found her attractive, and this was something for him to be very careful of because of who she was. It was not a wise attraction for the young Kane to be focusing his energies on. Even the most skilled enchantress wasn't a wise bet to be setting your sights on as a lover. Someone like Isra was truly damaged inside and probably not even capable of love So while attracted to her he was, it may well have served him to focus his attentions elsewhere.

Kane did indeed have a bride in his home village, but Lady Isra already knew that thanks to Romeo's gifted insight. Romeo had gladly told her everything and had predicted Kane's arrival. Because of that, Lady Isra of the Dark always went to Romeo when she needed help or advice on something.

So Lady Isra knew about Kane's bride, well, bride to be as they were engaged, but was puzzled why Kane had sought her help in making him God's gift to women when he already had one in his arms. Perhaps he just wanted to control her like most human men. He had been foolish in seeking the witch and this he now knew, but he hoped everything would be alright and prayed for the day when the witch would release him.

He forced a smile on his face and replied, "It sounds like a great experience. I hope it brings you to great things."

Lady Isra sat down next to Kane. "Yes, dear friend, it will indeed, many great things. It is a shame you will miss them, but I know you will do your best here while I am gone." Isra mustered before she left the room leaving him alone with his thoughts.

Kane looked terrified; she had just told him in her own terms to stay in line and do what she said. Yes, that surely was a threat. There would be hell to pay otherwise.

He shuddered and wondered what she would do next. He would have to be calm and patient now more than ever if he hoped to survive this.

17

Lady Isra awoke early the next day and told Kane she was not to be disturbed. He obeyed and stayed in the basement and was grateful she would not be near him for the time being as Isra was really starting to freak him out something awful.

It was something he did not need, as he was trying to stay calm and keep hope in his situation. After all, he was a prisoner in a witch's tower with no way out. How much calm and patience would someone need to get through a situation like that and still have hope?

Kane hoped he would have all he needed and said his prayers that he would be safely returning soon to his home village so he could marry his bride and forget this entire experience. By the time Kane had done all of his chores down in the basement, Lady Isra was gone. He did not know where she was or when she would be back; he was just glad to be free for now, at least.

Lady Isra had set off on a jolly walk in her new disguise, that of a kind old sweet lady dressed in rags and carrying a basket full of sweet delights, as most old ladies would. She had gone to a village a few miles away named Spindlevitch. Isra felt her old body inside her new false one and looked at herself in the mirror; gone was her long black hair with ringlets of curls and her stunning black lace corset dress.

She was now an old lady with a fraught and frail appearance, but had a sweet look about her, dressed in a ragged grey dress with patches of black sewn onto it. She looked cold, and her hands were wrinkled, but this was all right, as she was proud of her new appearance.

Just in front of her a jet-black raven was keeping watch on all that she was doing. In fact, he'd been incredibly clever to follow her here all the way from Shambre Fell but alas it was not his first attempt in staking out Lady Isra of the Dark. He was about to turn away and swoop up ahead when suddenly both of Isra's piercing green eyes glared upon him at that very moment. Feeling foolish Astrid the raven proceeded to fly off only to land haphazard in the holly bush that was adjacent to where he'd been perched to see Isra.

"What a peculiar little thing you are. Oh I do hope you are not hurt." Isra cooed, dropping down to her knees, bent down to get a closer look at the raven.

"Oh, how embarrassing," Astrid muttered as he swept himself off. "A bloody idiotic thing to do if I say so myself." Astrid continued as he found himself staring deep into Isra's eyes. Sure this horrid hag was staring at him but deep inside her saw her, jet black curls and all. *Why on earth is she wearing this bewildering disguise? It is most perturbing to me. Anyhow, all I have to do is shrug this off and hope I've gone fairly unnoticed.* Astrid conferred with himself as he knew that Isra catching him watching like this meant he was certain to be more careful now. He hadn't been that stealthy, thinking about it. But at least the witch seemed forgiving in the way she was stooped down trying to get a look at him. She was concerned for his welfare since he had landed on the prickly holly bush with quite the jolt.

"No. No. I am fine. Thank you kindly." Astrid replied in a formal tone. He didn't want to be rude, but it was important he got himself home now. He had already been spotted and he didn't need any more mishaps.

"Are you sure? You had quite the fall there." Isra inquired sweetly. Again she was in her old lady guise but still Astrid knew it was her. Deep down. There's no way she could ever hide her true form from him.

"Yes, I am fine. Thank you, my lady. And what a lovely day it is in Spindlevitch." He announced with a flair of interest.

"I love that name!" Isra retorted before she carried on examining the sights around her. Luckily whilst Isra's wandering eye got lost in the midst of this wholesome village completely distracted by this new place she hadn't noticed that her raven friend had skeddalled away.

Astrid took it upon himself to swan off into the skies so he'd be gone without trace but now Isra had seen him so as he sauntered into the cornflower blue mass among the shimmery white clouds he pondered something he hadn't considered for a long time. *Perhaps it is time for me to return.* It wasn't something he had honestly planned but Isra had seen him now. What possible benefit was there for him to keep ducking and diving around her like this? If he was going to be around her he needed to swoop back in as if he had never left. At least that was his reasoning around it.

Isra had already forgotten about the bizarre encounter she'd had with the raven. She was very interested in exploring her new surroundings. After all, Isra had come here to learn more about her slave boy, Kane, and was going to teach him a lesson for lying to her about what he had seen in the glass bowl. He had come from parents that were a gypsy and a seer, after all.

Isra stopped as she came across a tavern and looked through the windows and saw friendly villagers dancing, having fun, and drinking large tankards of beer. They looked happy for humans, so she decided this would be a good place to get a better look at the village. There was plenty of observing to do.

Isra stood by the door and slowly opened it. There were two behind a bar and some stools in front of the bar where people sat and drank their beverages. She carried on, further exploring this place, and to her right was an old man dancing around merrily to himself and singing.

To her left stood a perfectly proportioned maiden with long brown hair, a slim waist, a nice sized bosom and long legs. She wore a shimmery white dress with gold embroidery detailed in pleats down the sides of the dress. She stood on her own, chatting to some of the other people in the tavern and looked jolly, watching the others have a good time.

Lady Isra studied this young maiden carefully and thought to herself as she did so. *What a pretty young thing, so young, innocent and exquisite. I bet she has a lovely young man who looks after her.* She smiled as she inspected the young maiden who was now dancing with an older man.

But she did not see a man close to her. Sure, men danced with her, but Lady Isra could not see a soul that was connected to this young lady's soul. She wondered if she should explore this further.

Is this maiden Kane's bride to be? There was a very good chance she was, and Lady Isra had every intention of finding out more. Isra walked over to the young maiden and sat down on the stool next to her and asked, "Is this seat taken, dear?"

The young maiden smiled and said, "No, it is not, you go ahead and take it. You must be weary, being as old as you are."

Being as old as you are?! Haha, this maiden assumed that an old lady such as Lady Isra was frail and weak. Oh, big mistake, because she was not frail, even though her appearance for the moment certainly made it appear that way. Lady Isra remained calm at the insult.

"So, I bet a pretty young thing like you has a wonderful man to take care of her and be at your beck and call all day long. Where is this gentleman of yours, my dear?"

The maiden replied, "Yes. I have a man, and we are engaged to be married. He is away at the moment on a quest to find what he needs to benefit his life and ours. Kane is a great warrior and is always learning new things in his life."

Isra looked proud as she said this. Lady Isra took the maiden's hand. She had found Kane's bride, and it was easy, so easy, and she didn't even have to look that hard. She was a simple, sweet old lady in disguise, and she had found the beautiful young maiden without looking. Isra laughed at how easy it had been and licked her lips with delight. It had taken her less than a few hours to find this entrancing young lady of his and what a beautiful candescent soul she was too.

Isra studied the young maiden for a moment and paused; long black hair tied back, peachy fragrant skin, long white silk dress with gold trimming at the bottom and at the bosom to emphasize her slim figure with rosy cheeks. *Yes, this is the girl.* She had that innocent and unaware look about her. Innocent and yet also very naïve.

Kane had not told Lady Isra about his charming lady. In fact, when Kane came to Isra's tower seeking her; he had said he wanted women to fall at his feet, but yet he already had one? She laughed as she realized most human men wanted it all, never being truly satisfied with what they have.

It was getting late in the day, and the tavern was soon to close. The young maiden was clearing tankards away from the tables and piled them up, ready for washing. She noticed Lady Isra sat on the stool still and wondered where the sweet old lady would be headed.

She walked up to Lady Isra and said, "My dear lady, I hate to be rude, but where are you passing the night?"

Lady Isra straightened her old lady glasses upon her nose. "I do not know, my dear."

The maiden looked very serious for a moment. "You do not know? How so? You must have a place to pass the night! It can be very dangerous out there for a lady of your age to be wandering around with no safe place to go in the night."

Lady Isra smiled sweetly. "I am a traveler from another village. Do not concern yourself with my wellbeing, for I can take care of myself, despite my age."

"I am Lillian, and my home is near to here. You can stay there. Honestly, I would rather see you safe than left on these cold paved roads."

Lillian had clearly been fooled by her sweet exterior and had been taken in by the witch's strong but able personality. She knew little about anything really, and the witch saw that as she watched

Lillian talk with townsfolk in the tavern who were talking about things of interest, history, and Lillian clearly did not know.

Isra found Lillian dumb. Yes, that would be the best way of describing her. Not really knowing anything, but pretending to know anyway.

"Well, if you are sure I would be no trouble, I would be happy to accept your kind invitation." She smiled sweetly and pretended to struggle to open the tavern's heavy door.

Lillian gathered her things and prepared to leave and grabbed onto Lady Isra's arm and led her out of the door. She held a heavy lantern to light the way as they walked out into the dark night.

"By the way, I never heard your name?" Lillian asked Isra with a warm smile.

Lady Isra smiled and plainly replied, "Ivy. My name is Ivy."

18

They walked along the dimly lit path. Lillian lifted the hem of her dress to avoid getting dirt on it although that was inevitable considering all the dust that gathered on these narrow stone paths.

"My home is a little further from here, but I promise the journey does not take long. We just have to walk through a black wood. There is no civilization for a good two or three miles," Lillian said as she continued to hold on to Lady Isra's arm which irked Isra somewhat as she definitely didn't need a babysitter but she had to continue to play this role.

"That is fine with me; I like the dark," Lady Isra replied as she tried not to laugh, remembering that she was supposed to be a sweet old lady.

"Well, as long as you are sure. I promise you there will be a warm fire and hearth when we enter."

"That is all right, but are you sure, my dear?" Lillian paused for a moment at the question.

Was she sure? Sure of what? This new stranger was proving to be intriguing and also mysterious, but Lillian could not see a poor frail old lady out onto the street, so she did what any young woman would do; she took care of her elders.

It was such a shame that Lillian was not aware of who was really under the disguise. Because it was not a sweet, smiling old lady.

Lady Isra saw the perplexed look on the young woman's face. "Are you sure of your path in life, and that it is the right one for you, my dear?" She asked Lillian carefully.

Lillian felt the stare of Lady Isra burning into her. Lillian was happy in her life; she was going to be married, and despite many struggles that it had took to get her where she was now she felt content. Yet something from this stranger's words felt uncomfortable; something was not right.

Lillian felt uneasy, but how could she say such a thing to a sweet old lady? She had never felt uncomfortable around others before. She was a social person in the village and had many friends, many of whom would attend her wedding. She didn't hold grudges or bitterness. Never had she done so either.

Her journey to get to where she was right now in her life had been hard. She had been teased and ridiculed all throughout her schooling and felt out of place among the other pupils because of bullying. She had fought to find love, and when someone suggested to her to marry her long-term lover, Kane, who she had loved since a very young age, she could not wait to do it and immediately said yes when he proposed to her in the tavern.

They had a strong relationship, but she did not know about his affections for other women, and this made her quite naïve in many respects, as she let herself be walked upon by him on every occasion.

Sure, he loved her, and she loved him, but their relationship was not perfect, not by a long shot. Lillian always believed things would get better. Her parents got on well with Kane's parents, and so it was going to be a big family when their union would come to pass soon, and she could not wait for her dream to come true.

True love, like she had always wanted since a little girl. So, she had her struggles, but now she was ready to let go of all that and be happy with Kane. If only she knew his latest mission to seek learning and greatness had led to him being trapped in Lady Isra's tower and forced to become her slave. The worst part was that Lillian herself was now slowly falling for Lady Isra's trap and she had no clue.

They finally reached Lillian's cottage. She unlocked the gate, and they walked through the garden. The garden had red and white roses growing throughout it and lovely spring flowers in shades of orange and yellow and ivy growing around the walls. Lady Isra pondered on how nice and beautiful it all looked and how much love and care had gone into it.

Lillian welcomed Lady Isra in and made her some lemon tea before setting up a bed so she could comfortably pass the night. She unfolded the blankets and wrapped Lady Isra in one.

Lillian was curious about her new friend and wanted to get to know her, as she did with all the people she came across in her life.

She stared at Lady Isra for a moment as she drank her tea, then asked, "So, why are you here, Ivy? Do you have family nearby?"

Lady Isra smiled and replied, "No family here, no. My family died many years ago. I just came here to relax, and I am looking to set up home somewhere new. I do not know of many quiet villages, and this one had a nice feel about it. Do you have family here?"

Lillian gasped. "I am sorry to hear of your loss; I feel for you deeply as I have lost many people in my life. I am only close to my parents. Most of the family does not speak to us, but they are thrilled for my soon to be husband and me. We all speak and delight in each other's company, so that is a good enough family unit for me. I am looking forward to things."

"Well, that is good that you look forward, for there is no point in looking back," Lady Isra said quickly.

This caused Lillian to pause again and think about times when she and Kane were not as perfect as they were now. She thought to herself; *I wonder if I am doing the right thing. Does he truly love me?* Lady Isra had quite a profound effect on Lillian already and they had only met less than an hour ago!

Kane had come to her in strange circumstances. They had been thrown together at an early age, playing together in the forest and came to grow on each other and their love blossomed. She had been sixteen, and he was the same age as her.

Their courtship was swift but gradual; he wined and dined her at his parent's home, and soon she inherited the cottage from her grandmother. Kane took the opportunity for better things and moved himself in. He had a home of his own, of course, but he was always at loggerheads with his father, who wanted him to be a seer and use his gift to help others.

Kane was more interested in fighting and being a powerful warrior, so he and his father could no longer live in the same house. He persuaded Lillian to allow him to move into her grandmother's cottage, and because she was so in love with the idea of true love, she'd agreed.

He was there all the time, and she came home to him from her job at the tavern to find a home cooked meal and glass of wine made for her every evening. He did all he could to keep her happy, as deep down, Lillian was very insecure.

Lillian looked at the clock and said, "I must retire to bed now, but if you need anything, please let me know." She bid Lady Isra goodnight and went upstairs to her room.

Isra glanced at herself in the mirror and was relieved to see her younger appearance; of course, only she could see this. Humans could not, but if for instance there was a gifted person or another witch around, she could easily be discovered. Lady Isra was not worried about that, for she would not be there long. She would do what needed to be done and then she would return home to her tower.

She had been playing in this old lady disguise all day, and now she was pleased to see her true self.

She suddenly heard a tapping on the window and went to look as it grew louder. Someone clearly said her name.

"Isra, Lady of the Dark, come here, for I seek you."

19

———————

She walked over to the window and looked, and there before her was a raven. She had seen one before, but never up close except for that odd mishap earlier on in the village before she'd gotten to the tavern. The raven flew in the window and landed on her arm, looking up at her.

"Hello. I am a messenger from another land. I hear of your power and wish to assist you in any way possible. My name is Astrid, and I am at your service."

"Thank you but wait didn't I meet you earlier?" Isra inquired as she was sure that Astrid was the very same one that she'd noticed landing haphazardly in the bushes earlier on today.

"Aha, no sorry. There are a few of us around though!" Astrid dismissed her idea very swiftly. He didn't want to leave anything to chance. As far as Astrid was concerned he was making his grand entrance now. Because now more than ever presented the opportunity for him to come back. Why? He'd waited enough bleeding years had he not? Twelve years Astrid had waited for Lady Isra of the Dark. Everything on the light-bringer front had gone deathly quiet. And so he had deemed it was time to stop messing around and finally allow himself back into her life again. *What was*

81

the worst that could happen? Isra saying no? Telling him to buzz off. Please like she was going to do that! I've risked heaven and earth, well everything for Isra. Sure, she may not trust me but that's okay because I can gain that in time. I've waited bloody forever and a day for this. I can't bring myself to do it any longer. Staying away from her. It's killing me. Astrid went over this over and over inside his head. He'd wasted enough time. And let's face it, the light was hardly interested in Isra anymore but they might be if they knew what she was up to with this slave boy.

Isra looked over at Astrid with deep interest before she motioned, "Oh my apologies I was sure a raven identical to you approached me earlier but no matter." And she simply shrugged it off before pausing. He was quite the majestic character. Those deep beady eyes with the golden yellow sheen she was sure she'd seen it somewhere before. *I must be going mad.* Isra chorused in her thoughts as she left the thought drift away from her.

Lady Isra peered into Astrid's eyes inquisitively as she commented to him, "Why, you are a pretty thing! I am honored to have a friend such as you. Tell me, do you wish to share my power because some are afraid of me and what I do?"

Astrid squawked, then replied, "I am not afraid of you. I know you do dark things, but it is in your nature to be dark. This is truly what you are, and if others do not accept it, it is their problem, not yours. I am merely here to assist and guide you as you grow stronger."

Astrid leapt down from Isra's shoulder before he scooped a worm into his beak and asked, "So, do you plan on killing the girl?"

Lady Isra laughed. "The girl is a mere mortal, my friend, a poor maiden surrounded by drunk men. They will not miss her in this cruel and dreary human world."

"Hmm, you do whatever you see fit, and I will help in any way I can." Astrid advised her with a grin. *Goodness gracious. I was worried for nothing. Literally all it took for me to be in her bosom again was a simple greeting. Perhaps this will go much better than I had anticipated.* Astrid murmured to himself as he continued gobbling on the worm he'd just snapped up from the earth.

Isra smiled as she caught sight of her true form again. "Why, thank you, friend, but it is all under control. She believes I am a dear old woman, her friend. She will lead herself right into her own doom."

Although Lillian was easy to fool, the truth was Kane wanted to play away and have his cake and eat it. Lady Isra had discovered this when Kane came to her asking her to put a spell on him to make women fall over themselves to be with him.

Thinking about it for a moment, she wouldn't have to lead dear Lillian very far into a trap; she was already happily running along with her. She was naïve and did not think. Plus, she did not know that Lady Isra hid under the disguise she currently thought was her new friend. She looked at herself, white hair tied into a bun and her grey dress, worn and tired and fraying at the seams; she was frail and old, covered with wrinkles.

Lady Isra put down her mirror and looked at Astrid.

Astrid perched on the window ledge and gazed out as he replied, "Yes, the girl is easily led, it will be no trouble for you, I am sure. She will no doubt lead herself most of the way, if not all of it. She has a very innocent and yet also stupid look about her."

Isra laughed again and slyly remarked, "I should kill her just for being stupid enough to fall for it, really."

Astrid agreed. "Indeed, you should. Not that being stupid is a reason for death, but to not know of one's shortcomings is pure stupidity indeed."

Lady Isra heard footsteps coming from upstairs and quickly stood up and looked at Astrid. "You must go. The girl may wake up. I will talk to you soon."

Astrid smiled and prepared to say goodbye to his new friend. "It has been a pleasure talking to you, Lady Isra, and yes, you are quite right. We will do this again soon, sooner than you may think." He said to her with a wink.

And with that Astrid fluttered off, much abuzz in his own thoughts whilst Lady Isra closed the window as footsteps from above indicated that Lillian was making her way down the stairs.

Lillian saw Lady Isra sitting on the couch and smiled.

"Oh! I hope I did not wake you?" she asked softly.

Lady Isra smiled back at her and responded, "No, my dear, I sleep little these days. How come you are not in blissful sleep?" Isra asked Lillian with peaking interest. Isra had to be honest she hated this small talk lark but if she didn't engage with Lillian it would look suspicious so she had to keep up appearances.

Lillian paused for a moment and hung her head down as she explained to the witch, "I have terrible dreams. I fear they are to come true. I fear he may not return to me as he was."

Lady Isra silently cackled and smiled at her, taking Lillian's hand in her own as she recited, "Do not worry. Dreams are just the hidden doorways in the subconscious of our minds. Do not let fear take you over, for it is fear that holds you back the most in relation to what you seek."

Lillian looked confused for a moment, then replied, "But I do not fear, I know. I know something will go horribly wrong. I don't know how I know. I can just feel it. I have a lot of dreams like this, you see."

Lady Isra let go of Lillian's hand at once. "Perhaps we should have some tea?" Isra suggested. They'd certainly need something to lighten the mood. Isra was getting tired of Lillian's whining so she needed tea in any event.

Lillian nodded and went over to the kettle by the fire. Lady Isra watched as she poured the tea and smiled. Lillian nervously rushed along to give the cup to Lady Isra, and as Isra held it to her lips, she spoke.

"You are in a state of panic, my dear. You really must relax, for you cannot change the inevitable and you will only make it worse by worrying."

Lillian put on a smile and said, "Sorry. I am just a little nervous. This is the longest my lover and I have ever been apart. I worry about him ever so much."

Then she paused and looked at Isra. "What do you mean, the inevitable?"

Lady Isra sipped her tea as she explained in great detail to Lillian. "My dear, life is short. You don't extend it by worrying about things you cannot change; what will unfold soon enough. You will see what I mean."

Lillian looked puzzled. She thought about all kinds of chaos; her thoughts were expanding through her mind. Isra really had a good handle on this girl; she was controlling her without her even realizing. Lillian thought of Kane, and she thought of him coming back home only for him to tell her he was engaged to someone else.

The way his voice echoed in Lillian's mind was pure torture for her. She then saw a family gathering. Only everyone was in black, and everything was dreary. She guessed it was a funeral. Her thoughts were getting quite aggressive.

The next one was Lillian left alone in the forest, and she could hear someone calling her name in a deep voice, but she could not see who it was. By this point, she was very frightened and spilled the rest of her tea down her nightdress.

Isra hastily got up and went to reach for a cloth. Lady Isra got up and sat Lillian down and began pressing a cold cloth against her scalding legs with a wicked grin on her face as she did so.

It was almost time; the end was nigh.

20

Lady Isra dressed Lillian's burns and set out to make a fresh pot of tea as she calmly said, "You really must be more careful, dear. You've injured yourself badly. You must not worry so much; embrace what will be, let it swallow you whole."

Isra smiled as she handed Lillian a fresh cup of tea, and as Lillian took small sips, she asked sweetly, "So this lovely man of yours, why is he not here to help you with your worries and anxieties?"

Lillian straightened herself. "Kane is on a quest; he wants to find himself in life, make something of himself. He will be back soon, I hope."

Lady Isra asked, "What did you say his name was, my dear?"

Lillian finished her tea and replied proudly, "Kane. He is a warrior and son of a seer; he wants to do good in his life."

Lady Isra's eyes lit up immediately; she knew before, but now she had it confirmed again to her. She smiled an even more wicked smile than she had before. She had a plan unfolding in her mind, a brilliant one at that, but how to get Lillian to go along with it, well that would take some more time and thought. She was already doing a fantastic job of putting ideas into the poor girl's mind.

Lady Isra quickly added, "I know where he is, my dear. I have heard of him. He is in my home village."

Lillian gasped and said, "You know where he is? Please, can you take me to him? I miss him so very much; he brings so much joy to my heart."

Isra smiled and replied, "Yes, of course I can, but it is a long way away, and we must set off quickly. I know it is late, but we could get there by morning if we leave now."

Lillian got up and looked at herself in the mirror. She brushed her long brown hair before agreeing to the idea.

"Thank you, Ivy. I will dress myself, and then we will find Kane. I thank you ever so kindly for doing this; you are such a wonderful soul. Bless your heart."

Lady Isra heard the compliment clearly and simply smiled as Lillian rushed upstairs to get herself dressed and ready for the long journey ahead.

Yes, thank me kindly you will, she thought to herself wickedly, *and a wonderful soul, well, that I am not, but you find that out soon enough, my dear,* as she laughed to herself.

Lillian was falling for Isra's trap far too easily. Soon she was going to get revenge, and she was going to do it in such a way that nobody, not even Lillian or Kane, would see it coming. She loved it when things came together.

Isra wondered what Kane was doing. Little did she know, he was in her tower awaiting her return, as he had something to say to her. Kane sat down at Lady Isra's desk and sighed. He had been a prisoner for a few days, and with Lady Isra somewhere else, he wondered if he would ever get his freedom back.

Yes, the witch had been kind and spared him, but he wanted to be free. He pondered his situation for a moment as he looked out of the tower window, but at least he could see the sunshine outside dazzling brilliantly from the sky. He so desperately wanted to see it in person.

He wondered when Lady Isra would be back because he wanted to ask her for his freedom. He felt he had paid enough while he was here and now he wanted to go home, but the question was, would she let him?

Kane stared at an object on the shelf next to the window. It was an ordinary looking bookshelf, covered in dust and had many books on it, but what caught his attention was a raven statue he had not seen in the tower before. He thought he saw it move, but then he shrugged the thought off putting it down to his own cabin fever since he'd been holed up here for so long. At least a week now if he'd begun to count the days.

The statue was, in fact, Astrid monitoring Kane while Lady Isra was away, but Astrid was so still and quiet the slave boy had indeed thought he was a statue and not a friend of Lady Isra of the Dark.

Lady Isra and Lillian were just about ready to leave her grandmother's cottage. Lillian had put out the fire in the main room and had done the laundry. She wanted things ready for when she came back soon and with Kane, she hoped.

Isra was much less prepared as she had no intention of ever coming back to this place, although Lillian did not know it and was too busy thinking of Kane. She watched Lillian as she brushed her hair again and smoothed down the pleats of her white dress and admired herself in the mirror.

She put on a cloak. She wanted to look her best for Kane, and Lady Isra observed this in the way she presented herself and her frantic running around getting things.

Lady Isra admired herself as Ivy, for what she would be the last time, and smiled. She would soon deal with Lillian and then she would go back to her tower to confront Kane, but she was not sure how she would do it yet.

Oh well, there is plenty of time, she thought to herself. *Plenty of time for Lillian's demise and Kane's surprise.*

Lillian, now ready, shut the windows and closed the drapes. It looked poetic as Lady Isra looked on, patiently waiting for her to finish everything she was doing. It was like she was saying goodbye, which was ironic because Lillian would never return to this place again, but of course, she did not know that.

Lady Isra inspected herself in the mirror again. She looked pleased with herself; she had come all this way to find Kane's bride, and now she had her right where she wanted her. It was all worth it and all happening exactly as she had planned.

Then the moment came when they were finally free to leave. Lillian locked the door of the cottage and put the key in her dress pocket. Lady Isra watched as she took a deep breath and looked back at the rose garden before she made her way toward the gate to leave for what she did not know would be the last time.

Lady Isra took Lillian's hand, and they went down a dark pathway. It was getting dark, just about approaching dusk. Lillian looked nervously as Lady Isra guided her down the dark path. The trees were covering them as they walked.

Lillian would not get out of the forest alive, and Lady Isra knew it.

21

Lady Isra spoke to her coldly, "You must not be afraid of the dark, for the dark will know if you are. You must control your fear. If you do not, it will swallow you whole."

Lillian did not know what to make of Isra's statement. She was suddenly finding her new friend very unnerving, and she did not like it one bit. She turned to Lady Isra and asked her sullenly, "What do you mean my lady??"

Lady Isra laughed, cold as ice, in her reply. "Like all things, my dear, if you fear it, it will come for you."

Not quite understanding what Isra meant, Lillian asked, "So my fear will be the end of me?"

Lady Isra laughed again, this time a little louder than before, and answered, "Yes, my dear. If you allow it to control you, your fear becomes your reality."

Lillian smiled inquisitively and said, "My fear becomes my reality if I allow it to be so? That is interesting. I have never heard of a philosophy like this before."

Lady Isra paused and thought to herself, *No, dear, that is not a philosophy you have heard of before, because you do not stop to think and see what is going on around you.*

The path they were walking down had now become darker, and they could hear the eerie voices in the trees, whispering many lovely things. Lady Isra heard them and laughed as Lillian shuddered. This girl feared pretty much anything, and it amused Isra how fearful she was.

She shuddered again as they walked further and further down the dark path. There were no lights at all, and they traveled only by the tiny lantern in Lillian's hand; the other one, of course, was being held forcefully by Lady Isra of the Dark. Lady Isra's piercing green dragon eyes lit up the entire path right in front of her.

Lillian heard a scream, and she turned around to see what it could be but couldn't see anything.

Lady Isra laughed and said, "It is the forest, my dear. You will hear all sorts at night, Iit is best to keep moving. We have a long way ahead of us."

Lillian nodded and agreed. "Yes, you are right, Ivy, but I do hope we get somewhere less dark soon. I dislike this place very much."

Lady Isra sneered. Her voice was colder than ever, and her eyes narrowed. "It does not like you either, but we must make the best of things. Come."

Lillian looked at Lady Isra in horror for the first time. Who was this woman she was trusting to lead her off into darkness? Why was she being like this, so cold toward her?

She realized it was no longer Ivy holding her hand; it was Lady Isra herself in her full glory, a slender but beautiful woman with black curly hair and piercing green eyes.

Lady Isra smiled and said, "Is everything alright, my dear?"

Lillian gasped. "Where is Ivy??"

Isra smiled her most sinister smile ever as she cackled with insincerity. "Stupid girl, Ivy is a figment of your poor weak human imagination, but she did a good enough job, didn't she? Now we must go. Someone is waiting for you."

Lillian was not taking this too well; her friend had changed and turned on her, literally. The lovely old lady she had met in the tavern was long gone and in her place stood a beautiful and yet also dark enchantress who she did not feel comfortable with, and she did not want to go anywhere with her.

"I do not wish to go anywhere with you. Where is Kane?" Lillian demanded to know.

Lady Isra said, "He is waiting for you, but we must hurry if we are to get to him in time. He is in a bit of trouble, for he has messed with a witch!!"

Lillian looked terrified. Her face turned a pale white color and exclaimed in horror, "A witch? There is no such thing!"

"Yes, my dear, your beloved Kane came to my very tower and asked me to cast a spell on him to make the women of the world fall over themselves with love and devotion for him. He did not see what he had in front of him. Your beloved does not love you," she finished softly.

Lillian slowly fell to the floor, for she was in shock. Shocked that Kane, her dearest love, had sought help and love from other women, she held onto a tree for support as she fell hard as the truth sank into her very soul.

"He came to you asking for the devil's help? Do you work with the devil?" she asked as Lady Isra laughed again.

I always believed that witches worked with the devil, but Lady Isra did not know of the devil enough to believe in him or not. She had heard of that rumor for many years, as she lived in isolation. However, like most things, she ignored it, for it was the word of pathetic humans with their fear and weaknesses. She did not believe in the devil, but she had her demons; she did not need to believe in a manmade fabrication.

She turned to Lillian and replied sweetly, "No. I do not work with the devil, nor do I know him. I have my source of power, and it is far greater than anything a human could fabricate. So are you coming or not?" Isra quizzed Lillian as she was getting more tired by the second.

Lillian did not seem sure of herself. Lady Isra saw this as an opportunity and stood before Lillian and muttered some words under her breath.

Lillian wasn't aware Lady Isra stood silently in front of her with a dagger.

Isra swiftly slid it across Lillian, cutting her all over her body. In a matter of seconds, she was dead. Her neck was slashed, her breasts were cut on both sides and by her heart. She dug her dagger further into Lillian's chest and removed her heart.

Laughing, she said, "You will not need this again, my dear. Oh, don't you look beautiful?"

She had fulfilled her well laid plan, and she was delighted.

22

She heard something behind her and turned to see what it was. Lady Isra stood listening; she knew she was not alone in the forest, so she tuned in for a moment and blissfully listened to everything around her.

Suddenly, something landed on her shoulder. She realized it was Astrid, who had been monitoring Kane while she was away.

Astrid cawed loudly. "I see the deed is done. Her mortal soul will be in peace now, but the question is: are you?" He looked at his friend with much concern in his eyes.

Lady Isra smiled and calmly announced, "Peace will come, but first Kane needs to see what has become of his beloved. He will regret this for the rest of his pitiful human life."

Astrid cawed again. "Did she scream?" he asked.

Lady Isra paused and thought for a moment and let her mind go back to Lillian's demise. *It had been too quick for the poor girl to be in any pain.*

"No. I swooped over her and cut her heart out. She didn't feel it, but even if she had, it wouldn't have been for very long. Her sacrifice was a fast one."

Astrid smiled and said, "Well, the boy is blissfully unaware of anything, but I listened to him as he was voicing his thoughts. He wants you to let him go."

Lady Isra found this rather amusing and laughed loudly. It was too ludicrous to believe. "Let him go?!" she exclaimed.

"Yes, he feels he has paid enough debt to you and wants his freedom." Astrid explained to Isra with a blank expression. He had no idea how Isra would react so he was being cautious.

"Oh, I will let him go alright, I'll let him go into the darkest, deepest pits of Hell, and he can find freedom once he is down there." Isra retorted with a hint of annoyance in her voice.

Astrid continued, "Well, I guess the next move is to return home and keep him waiting?"

Lady Isra smiled and looked down at Lillian's lifeless body, thinking about the task at hand. "We need to take this poor thing with us. She needs to be near her beloved Kane. Oh, the wondrous treat I have in store for him!" she replied evilly.

Astrid moved closer and inspected the body, sniffing it a little. "Hmm, I guess we should make a start now if we are to get there by daybreak."

Isra paused for a moment and remembered that near the tavern, there was a horse drawn carriage that she could use to transport herself and Lillian back home and not be seen by any townspeople. Not that she was worried about getting noticed by any of them.

"There is a carriage near to where I first met her; we shall use it to travel home."

Lady Isra studied Lillian again and smiled. She then realized she was still in the grey ragged dress she had worn since she became Ivy. Isra ripped it off her and closed her eyes for a moment and envisioned herself in a black energy surrounding her entire being.

She opened her eyes to find herself in a long black dress with lace on the arms and lace pleats down the side. She admired herself, taking extra care to notice the lace sleeves that generously covered half her arms and stood back in awe at how perfect she looked.

Isra walked over to Lillian and looked poignantly upon the girl. Isra stood before Lillian and whispered some words, and in her mind saw Lillian becoming smaller, as if she could fit in her palm. Once this was done, Lady Isra put Lillian in her pocket.

She turned to Astrid and announced, "Right, let us go home, friend, she is ready to be transported."

Lady Isra traveled many miles to get back to the tavern where she had first met Lillian with Astrid perched on her shoulder, humming to himself. After a few hours, they arrived at their destination just as it was getting light outside. It was dark and empty inside; nobody was there. The sun was about to rise as the moon had just died in order to bring the new day.

Isra smiled as she noticed the empty glasses and tankards. No one had been here for days and as for Lillian, her job there was long over. She stepped into the carriage, and off they rode with Lady Isra in the back and Astrid still perched on her shoulder.

Isra had grown to like her new friend and his company very much. Astrid had also been keeping a watchful eye on Kane while Lady Isra was away doing her business with Lillian. She was grateful to Astrid; he did what she needed and had not asked her for anything. He was monitoring Kane because it interested the witch and he was here to look after her interests. After all, Astrid was incredibly invested in Isra but she didn't know the full story at all did she?

They'd traveled a long way and arrived by noon. Lady Isra stepped out of the carriage and smoothed her dress as she stared at the sun. It was a lovely day, and it could only get better. She looked up at the window of her tower and thought of Kane, of how she would torment and torture him soon; all in the mind, of course, but still very fun anyhow.

She approached the main tower door and turned the key. Astrid flew in after her, and she climbed the stairs and unlocked the other door, listening carefully to make sure Kane was not behind it.

Kane, in fact, was in the basement. But she walked in briskly and watched as Astrid flew around her, excited for the day's festivities, and perched upon a skull on the bookshelf.

Lady Isra shouted, "Kane, Kane, Kane!"

At once, the slave boy Kane came into the room and stood in front of Lady Isra. "You called, my lady?" he replied.

"Yes. I did. I trust you are well?" she inquired as she moved her eyes over him, checking for signs of dishonesty and fear.

He seemed a little shaky but no dishonesty so far, which was good for now. She continued staring at him as she waited for his answer.

He looked at her and replied, "Yes, I am well, my lady, but I wanted to ask you a question, if I may?"

She looked at him again; what could he possibly want to ask her?

She knew already he wanted his freedom, but he would not get that, not until he had seen what had happened to dear old Lillian.

23

Kane was still looking shaky as he looked at the witch with pure fright and fear at what he was about to ask. He wanted the words to come out perfectly, but they did not. Instead, they came out rather fast, which made him seem incredibly rude and arrogant as he uttered them.

"I feel I have served enough time here and wish you to let me go, Lady Isra." Kane stated clearly. He had obviously thought of this for some time while Isra had been away as it had sounded rehearsed.

She looked at him and laughed. It was not a good omen when she did this because it meant she could well be mocking him, which she was going to be doing shortly, but alas that was a surprise, a very well laid one. Lady Isra finally spoke and seemed sincere when she made her response.

"Well, if that is what you feel, I shall have to take it into consideration, Kane, but one more thing before I do. Have you ever lied to me, dear?" she asked as he turned a harsh shade of white.

He had gone incredibly pale. Kane stared at Lady Isra of the Dark, his mouth wide open, and he looked at her in sheer terror. She had just asked him the one thing he did not want to be asked. He looked at her and attempted to look calm.

"No. I have not; I would not do that." He lied through the tension that was surging through his body.

She looked at him wickedly and stayed calm. "I would hope you have not, my dear, for I do not take kindly to liars. They grate the very core of my being."

Oh dear, she knew, she knew all along. Kane mumbled in his thoughts.

She must have seen him when he saw the vision in the bowl of water. Kane was left reeling from her response. How on earth was he going to get out of this? *She knows, she fucking knows! What else does she know?*

He had well and truly pissed off Lady Isra of the Dark, but he did not know what she had in store for him. Kane still looked terrified but had handled the interrogation. She had just done with him well. He was a little weak from all the fear.

She had only said a few words to him and totally had him there and then. He was more than scared but tried his best not to show it. He had retreated and gone back to his chores in the basement.

Lady Isra casually sat with Astrid perched on her shoulder in her main room, drinking tea and perusing through one of her books. She was happy and content with the situation and was taking some time to relax. Having already killed Lillian and making Kane squirm, she decided that now was a good time to catch up on her reading.

Astrid also seemed happy as he sat on her shoulder and hovered over her, keeping an eye out for anyone or anything that might disturb or intrude upon them. Astrid was very protective of the witch. He had felt like he had known her before, so he wanted to make sure she was safe, even though a mighty powerful witch would always be safe, but in his way, he wanted to make sure of it. He cared for her and her interests, not lovingly, but more like a protective, friendly brother kind of way.

Astrid was happy to do all she wanted to get rid of Lillian and was now serving her again, watching Kane, who was quivering in the basement after he had asked the witch for his freedom, and in no uncertain terms, she'd rejected his request to be free.

Of course, she had lots planned for Kane, but he would find out about these things soon enough. She wanted to let him sweat a little first. She enjoyed it, but perhaps she enjoyed it a bit too much.

Kane sat in quiet solitude pondering his situation and thinking to himself. *How am I ever going to get out of this alive?*

Kane wanted to be free. He wanted to get out of his mess in one piece. He just didn't know how. He had hoped for a miracle but being Lady Isra's prisoner; he was quite short of miracles right now. Kane thought of how things were back at home in his village; then his mind wandered to his terrible fate again. He was truly at a loss, and he didn't know what to do.

Then he suddenly heard a noise from the window. It was coming from outside. He listened carefully to see where it might come from. He could not open the window, as Lady Isra had put iron bars all around it so he could not escape. He could see clearly through the bars, and there was Romeo the python on the window ledge.

Romeo laughed as he peered through the window at the queer human and chuckled, "Dear me, what mess have we got ourselves into here? Is there a way out? That, we do not know but there is only one way this can go."

Kane looked at the green snake and replied, "Great, a talking snake. That's all I need. You are no help to me. You are friends with the witch, so why would you want to help me?"

Romeo uncoiled himself and sighed as he said, "I cannot help you, young man. You need to help yourself. You got yourself into the mess, and now you must get out of it."

Kane sighed. "I do not know how to get out of it. I am in real deep trouble, gone too far this time I have; she will not let me go. I fear I will never get out of here."

Romeo looked at Kane and sighed again. He then questioned Kane. "Oh, my goodness, what have you done to upset Lady Isra now? She is blackened to the core, her heart is surely rotten, but any misdeeds against her will not go unforgotten."

Kane paused as he beseeched Romeo in frustration, "Please, dear sir Romeo, stop talking in riddles! Tell me, how am I to fight the witch?"

Romeo sighed and uncoiled himself further from his branch. "You cannot, my young man. Lady Isra is immortal and, therefore, cannot be harmed. You made your mistake; now you must live it and pray she spares your life." Of course, Romeo did not know Lady Isra had tracked down Kane's bride and left her bleeding to death in the forest. Kane was in for one hell of a surprise, and she had every intention of making him pay for his betrayal.

24

He heard something; this time it was singing. He looked out the window again, and Romeo was singing a rhyme so all could hear, maybe even Lady Isra. He was singing in riddles, and he grew louder and louder as Kane listened.

"Her heart is no longer pure; she knows that for sure.

She stays in her blackened shell, knowing all is well.

Do not breathe, do not shake.

She's been to Hell, and back, don't bother to cut her any slack.

She will happily send you death and Hell, and you won't suspect a thing,

You will think it's all butterflies and fluttering wings.

She shines in the darkness and dances at night; she could give you quite a fright.

But remember, just when you think she could be good again,

She'll go even further down the line to even more darkness and dazzling shine."

Kane realized Romeo was talking about Lady Isra. He'd said her heart was no longer pure. Kane felt she took advantage of that, especially as she seemed to love being evil, or maybe that was just part of her.

Then he focused on the part where he'd said Lady Isra would happily send death and Hell and you won't suspect a thing; yes, she was very good at that. She could make things seem fine when really all Hell was breaking loose, and everything was sheer chaos.

This was making him more nervous about the witch, but Romeo didn't have to give him this insight. In fact, it was getting a little unclear just whose side Romeo was on as he was believed to be a companion of Lady Isra's, but perhaps not as much of a companion as he had first thought if he will give Kane such a remarkable piece of insight.

Kane pondered on this advice, and when he went back to the window to thank Romeo, he noticed the green python had totally disappeared, gone without a trace. But his work was done. If Romeo and Lady Isra were indeed not as close as she thought, then the witch had not suspected a thing. She still trusted Romeo's advice and insight whenever she consulted with him, but the last time she had been before her trip to Kane's village, so it had indeed been a long time.

Suddenly, Kane heard Lady Isra calling him from the basement. He hastened away from the window and answered her call.

"You called, my lady?"

She smiled sweetly and replied, "I have thought about what you said and figured you may appreciate some time outside on the grounds of the tower today. I have a task for you if you are willing and able to do it for me."

Kane pondered for a moment and answered, "Yes, I would like that. What is it you wish for me?"

Lady Isra licked her lips and smiled. Taking the slave boy's hand, she replied, "Come with me, and I will show you."

She led him out the door, outside to the grounds of the tower, and with the look on her face, who knew what deadly treat was in store for him? Surely it couldn't be anything good. Lady Isra did nothing that was good.

Kane looked on as she led him down a small pathway, then into an area surrounded by trees and flowers. She let go of his hand and smiled at him. She pointed toward a patch in the middle, covered in flowers.

"Kane, I am looking for a particular flower for a spell I'll soon be doing. It is a black rose, said to be powerful. I need you to be careful while looking for it, but look for it. You must, as it is essential to my spell work. Questions?" Kane looked at the area and looked at the trees, then looked back at Lady Isra as he responded with a new ray of hope. "No, my lady. I think I understand what is required of me. I will do my best to retrieve the flower for you."

Isra watched closely as Kane looked at the flowers, paying close attention to several bushes which also had flowers on them too. Deep red and burgundy roses cohorted with several of them in mauve and violet but there wasn't a glimmer of a jet black rose to be seen anywhere which Isra had known since she was the only person who tended to the garden in the grounds of Shambre Fell.

A black rose? Oh, no... why does that sound familiar. Oh, my. Astrid chorused to himself in thought but then he let himself remember. He couldn't explain to Isra how he knew this because her memories had been taken however in time, he hoped that she would be able to remember all they had shared. For now, all he could do was enjoy the moment with her. It was perplexing to Astrid how Isra was making Kane search for a black rose when Astrid knew it was connected to a prophecy surrounding Isra that had not yet come to pass.

Astrid landed on her shoulder and observed the scene and laughed. "He must think this is his lucky day, getting out in the grounds. So close to freedom, but yet he won't be able to touch it." He watched the slave boy just as closely as Lady Isra had been doing.

Lady Isra looked at Astrid and laughed. "That pathetic human being has no chance of freedom; he won't even get to sniff it, my dear. Come, let us watch him some more."

The pair watched as Kane went about his business, taking care to notice every flower and plant that was there, taking each one by the stem and carefully lifting its petals to see what was underneath them. The witch sat upon a chair nearby while Astrid perched on her shoulder, his beady eye watching every move the slave boy made.

Kane, however, was struggling with his task. He looked at the flowers, but he could not see a black rose. He looked among all of them; there were many colors, green, pink and red and other colors among those, but not a single one of them was black. He got anxious. His search was leading him nowhere, but he remained somewhat optimistic. It was all he could be at a moment like this.

It has to be here; he thought to himself. *I must find it. What will happen if I don't? Surely the witch will kill me! I hope she doesn't, but if I fail, she may very well. I must work harder. I must find it.*

Lady Isra laughed. She was going to have more fun with this boy, and he was about to find out just how far her form of mental torture could go. Astrid whispered merrily, "That boy won't get out of here alive, will he?"

Lady Isra giggled wickedly. "He will live. He will have no choice but to live, my friend. That is the curse of human life," she said with a mischievous look on her face.

Astrid admired Isra in that moment. He genuinely liked her for what she truly was. He didn't just admire her; he respected her, and few can say that about a witch. She had that lure about her that reeled you in from the first moment, and he liked the way she operated, as well. She didn't like betrayal, and if anyone did that or any other such thing, she wouldn't hesitate in taking revenge, and he liked that very much. Her personal prowess and strength was one of the qualities that had attracted him to her in the first place.

Astrid leaned close to Lady Isra's ear and said, "Well, I know you well enough to know you will do as you see fit, and if that includes taking this one as far as it can go, well you go right ahead and do it, my friend."

Lady Isra cackled. "Evil is all around, my friend. It spawns from where it stems and all those humans trying to do right think they are making a difference. The sad truth is they are not. Their efforts are a failure because eventually, the darkness that lies in them all will reach out and grab them, so why not accept what is inevitable and make it happy?" She laughed again and added, "That boy hides from all things dark, but I have a special treat in store for him."

Who knew what this special treat could be? Kane's ordeal was far from over.

Kane still had not found a black rose. He had been there for some time, wondering why he could not find one. After all, it was just a simple black rose. It shouldn't have been too hard to find, but alas, it had stumped the boy. Probably because it didn't exist in the first place.

25

Lady Isra had decided Kane had enough freedom for today and went out to the grounds, with Astrid swiftly following her. She sweetly asked Kane, "Any luck finding my black rose?"

Kane looked at her and hung his head in shame. "No, my Lady. I cannot find it anywhere. I have searched very hard but to no avail." He shuffled his feet and waited for Lady Isra's response.

The witch responded evilly, "Very well, Kane. You have indeed tried your best, but perhaps you should get back to the basement and get on with your chores. You have had enough time outside for today."

Kane dutifully agreed and went back into the tower, followed by Lady Isra who was quick to lock the main door behind her. Kane was trapped, and she was making sure of it. She had given him a taste of his freedom, only to take it away as quickly as she had given it. It was a very spiteful and mean trick, but it gave her great pleasure.

Back in the basement, Kane couldn't understand why he had failed in his task of finding the black rose. The witch had given him explicit instructions. Despite that, he could not find it. He thought

Lady Isra may have been mad at him for not finding it, but she seemed pretty thrilled, in fact.

The witch sat in her tower, casually spread out on her couch, drinking honey tea while reading one of her books. Astrid rested on her shoulder, singing sweetly in her ear. She was in an excellent mood, and Kane's misery had made it so good. She loved reveling in the misery of humans; it made her feel amazing.

She had been thinking of her friend Romeo and was getting somewhat nostalgic about it; she remembered the first time they met and how friendly he was. Romeo had introduced himself to her almost immediately, and he'd said he knew about her power and how dark she was and had come to her as a friend.

He'd told her that a man would come to seek her out from the human world, and soon after Kane had arrived at her tower. He had seen Lady Isra kill the dragon, and he had seen her take the power inside herself. Romeo also had seen her blackened heart.

Romeo had come to Kane and warned him of Lady Isra while uttering a cryptic rhyme about the witch, but Lady Isra did not know this. If she did, she may not have been thinking of getting in touch with Romeo. She finished her honey tea and waited until Kane was sound asleep in the basement before she then made her way down the stairs and ventured off into the night with Astrid, who was fast becoming a most beloved companion of the dark mistress.

The air was crisp and clear, and Lady Isra felt there was a special chill upon the night. The forest was deserted as she made her way through the clearing in the trees. She continued to bask in her dark surroundings. She wandered the path for some time before finding Romeo's tree. The stars glittered with extra sparkle and lit the pathway.

She knocked on the trunk and called out softly, "Dear Romeo, are you here?"

For a few moments, there was nothing; no rustling in the tree, no movement coming from above. She looked up to see if there were any signs of life from the top, but alas, nothing. As she turned to walk away, a voice stopped her.

"Well, if it isn't, Lady Isra of the Dark comes to visit the reptilian species as we supposedly sleep while the night keeps us young and healthy."

Lady Isra turned around and smiled at the voice of her old friend, and she happily announced, "Why dear Romeo, it has been a long time. How are you? It's a beautiful night. I trust it is treating you well."

The snake made his way down the tree and perched himself on a branch just near enough to see Lady Isra.

Romeo smiled as he uncoiled himself. "It is always treating me well here. How are you? I have not seen you since your grand trip."

"Ah, that. It was a beautiful day of learning, and I learned a lot from it."

She had a sparkle about her tonight. A happy vibe. It was almost like she was shimmering all over. She was so blissfully happy he could see her green eyes, piercing as they normally were, but sparkling like the stars. Her long curly black hair also had a touch of sparkle about it. She was a powerful and mystical being, and this symbolized to Romeo that a transformation was taking place despite the darkness.

Romeo looked deeper into the witch's eyes to see if he could see what was causing the glimmer and delight that he was feeling from every inch of her being. He knew something had changed; he just wasn't able to pinpoint what.

It wasn't love. It couldn't be love. Someone as dark and evil and full of power, someone who enjoyed using that power to its full potential to destroy and ruin all that they touched, could never be capable of love and loving another. He knew this, but something told him that Isra was different.

Something about her had changed, but again, he did not know what. He decided the best course of action was to question the witch, for if she were glowing, she would surely tell her serpent friend exactly what was behind her glow, wouldn't she?

He looked at her again. "A beautiful day of learning? My, and what did you learn, my lady?"

Lady Isra held a tree branch and looked at it with great deep love and affection, like nature had suddenly become a lot brighter and sweeter to her. Now that her revenge had been exacted upon Kane, it was as though she could happily go about with life in her stride and admire its extraordinary beauty and hidden magic.

"Oh, I learned a lot. The humans float through their lives waiting for hope, and it really is quite beautiful. They put all they can into hoping and praying that every- thing will be okay and turn out wonderful. When it doesn't, when that hope is taken from them, it's like a rush watching that diminishes and disappears. Then their pain comes. I've never seen that before. It was new."

Romeo paused and asked, "You got pleasure from this learning experience?"

Lady Isra looked deep into Romeo's eyes. "Yes, my friend. I never understood humans, nor do I have much time for them, but you have to admire the beauty of the pain they go through. It is inspirational."

She paused and licked her lips. "I mean, I'd never done it before, and wow! You can't imagine how it feels. It was amazing."

Isra relived the experience in her mind over and over, the images so satisfying as they replayed in her mind. Not the brutal end that she'd served to Lillian but the fact that she'd gotten one over on a man who had tried to win her over for reasons that he'd never be able to forget. *A man's foolishness is seldom very well-seasoned. But one must always remind ourselves that eventually the lesson comes and hopefully they live to appreciate it the next time around.* Isra perused the notion to herself as she had hoped Kane would realize he had made a most fatal mistake in tracking her down.

26

———————

Romeo wasn't truly understanding Isra but it had seemed to him as though she'd gained something incredible from her extracurricular activities.

Romeo then pondered the question to her, "So, you have learnt a lot about the humanity of others? My, you have come far into the world. No wonder the stars shine on you tonight. You are glowing."

Lady Isra laughed. "Yes, it was a dark night like this one, and this particular human was squirming and realizing all her hopes had turned to nothing. She truly loved that man, even though he betrayed her by wanting more than what she was giving him. I knew humans were weak, but this one was special. It just shows you no matter what they have, it still isn't enough for them."

Romeo replied, "I see. So you studied the girl and then left her to marinate. How very interesting."

He clearly had some reservations about this news from Lady Isra. It seemed as though Isra was detailing something that far was more immaculate than what it had sounded like however she was being vague on the details which irked Romeo somewhat, but he could see the difference in Isra's demeanor.

"Yes, it was. I'd never understood the true facets of human life

III

before." Isra replied earnestly.

Romeo took another look at Lady Isra of the Dark again; she had become something truly great. That caused her new shining glow. Her unique sense of power and beauty. She had taken something so remarkable. Now her life would never be the same ever again.

Romeo asked, "What is next for you, my lady? More learning experiences by cohorting with the humans?"

Lady Isra smiled wickedly. "Only if there needs to be. My dear slave boy doesn't know what's happened, but I think he needs to know soon. He knows he made a terrible mistake in seeking me out, but he doesn't know just how bad that mistake was. Not yet."

Romeo could see how this was going to pan out. He felt a little sorry for the slave boy as he realized Lady Isra was for sure going to lead him to whatever she's done but she would do it in a sweet and also beautiful but yet caring way he thought as she said the word that told him that Kane's demise would arrive soon. His ordeal was not over yet. The poor human, he thought, seeking a witch for the magic and now that dastardly deed would return to haunt him as his torture was not over yet.

Romeo looked on and replied, "I am sure when the time comes, you will do what you feel is necessary as I know you to be very swift and severe for dealing with humans. He will live to regret ever hearing your very name."

Lady Isra listened to that last sentence carefully; it was almost prophetic. **He will live to regret hearing your very name.**

It wouldn't be long before poor Kane would find out why. But she could wait a little longer for that perfect, beautiful moment.

Romeo and Lady Isra had been talking for several minutes, and it was getting late. Romeo had heard enough, so he finally said, "Well, my lady, I must bid you a good night, as I have things to do in the morning. It was nice to hear from you. Come again, friend."

Lady Isra smiled. "Oh, you will see me soon. Have no fear of that, sweet Romeo."

She said goodbye to him and made her way back home. Astrid flew by her side, and the witch paused as she heard a noise behind her. She stopped in her tracks and tuned in with the surrounding area to see what it might be.

She smelled the air and closed her eyes for a moment and listened. She had long done this to quieten herself and connect with everything around her; it had been a great asset in her craft to have that much needed focus and concentration.

Although it was dark, the witch could see very well, and in the distance, a figure emerged from what seemed like a plant, an overgrown shrub. The flowers on it were dried up and dead, which Lady Isra didn't find unnerving as she was used to things of this nature manifesting when something ghastly was lurking in the vicinity.

The figure came closer, and she saw it was a woman, covered by a dark cloak and holding a small lantern in her hand. She approached Lady Isra and spoke, her voice worrisome and desperate. The witch could smell her fear, and it also reflected in her ragged appearance.

"I am looking for my son. He came here to find something, and he has not returned home. We are all anxious for him," she said as the witch studied the woman carefully.

Lady Isra knew at once this was Kane's mother. She suppressed her laughter, remembering the poor woman standing next to her.

She straightened and said, "Oh my, what a terrible thing to happen. Tell me, what is his name? "

The woman removed the cloak from her head to reveal a head of red hair and a worn, tired face. "Kane; he is tall, wavy blond hair and of good stature."

Lady smiled. "Sorry. I have not seen him, but few men come to these parts of the land. I bid you well as I have to get home, but I hope you find him."

And with that, Lady Isra took off with a big grin on her face; it was almost time. Kane's mother, however, was searching all over the forest. Astrid had been keeping watch on the woman as she searched for her poor boy. If only she had looked closer. She had traveled a long way to find her beloved son, but the search would soon prove to be a failure.

27

Lady Isra was in a superb mood after meeting Kane's mother and was planning her next move. She was going to exact her revenge soon, much sooner than she had planned. Kane's mother had given her inspiration and motivation. Even though she had been looking forward to this for some time, she was now psyched up to do it.

Oh, he is going to learn; she thought to herself. *He will never do something like this again.*

Back in her tower, she joked with Astrid about the poor woman who was soon to find her son was never coming back. Astrid was in good spirits too, as he had kept an eye on the woman and had watched her crying.

"Poor old hag, she will never find him," Astrid said profoundly. He had wanted to bring up a primitive matter but had swiftly decided against it as he would not be able to fill in the blanks when Isra would ultimately bring up further questions about it. Isra knew nothing about the black rose or the prophecy surrounding it. It would only cause her confusion for him to bring it up now and he'd only just came back to her. It would have to wait.

Lady Isra looked at the raven with much love and admiration. She had grown to love her dark feathered companion, and now she could not be without him. Isra knew from her experiences that love was something that could only exist in dreams, but she had long stopped that dream. Now she was who she was, and she loved it, but she didn't have love in her heart and had grown to accept that.

"Oh, Astrid, her search is a failure, and the poor woman knows it, hahaha! She will find out in time, my friend, she will find out all in time." They both suddenly heard noises coming from the basement.

She turned to Astrid and said quietly, "Perhaps we should go check on the young man downstairs?"

Astrid nodded, and Isra went out of her main door and slowly climbed down the staircase to the basement where Kane was currently dwelling. Astrid followed as she entered the basement and softly called out Kane's name.

"Kane, oh Kane, come here."

Kane heard the witch's voice and got to his feet at once. He walked over to her and bowed before her, which she liked. He was desperate now, really desperate, but that didn't stop him from trying to find a way out of this. Kane's spirit had been crushed by Lady Isra once again.

The last time he'd had contact with her, she had sent him on an impossible task, giving him a taste of freedom for her to only take it away again once he failed miserably.

She smiled sweetly at his bowing to her and said, "Ah, there you are, my dear. You have been awfully quiet. I just wanted to check on you to make sure all is well."

By being sweet and kind, she was confusing Kane's brain, and that she liked, she enjoyed messing with his mind. She was going to do a lot more than mess with his mind soon enough, although he had no clue of that just for the moment.

Kane replied quickly, "I am fine. Is there anything you want me to do?"

Lady Isra considered his question. "Actually, for now, you are fine.

Just stay here and do your chores, which I presume are being done to the highest standard, yes?"

Kane looked down at the floor, and when he could see his reflection in it, he looked relieved. "Yes, all done to your high standards, my lady."

She looked satisfied at his response. "Ah, very good. I will leave you to your work. I am going out for a while, but I will be back before dawn."

Isra was increasing her mental torture on Kane as the days went by, and it became more sinister every time she inflicted it upon him. Just a simple trick of the mind, reinforcing her punishment on him by reminding him he was here, and he had work to do.

She may as well have said, "You are here, and this is your life now and always will be."

It was brilliant, and she was pleased with herself with it, but she was really gearing herself up to torture him soon. She was just waiting for her moment and then she was going to really show him what a mistake he had made.

It was getting close to light, and Lady Isra ventured out for the night and take her beloved Astrid with her. It was a cool, clear night, and she enjoyed being out in the woods with just her friend for company. Nature had a way of soothing her soul, not that she rarely needed soothing.

Everything was quiet; she could almost hear a pin drop. She walked amongst the trees as Astrid, perched on her shoulder, quietly hummed in her ear. He was a very peaceful soul himself, despite being drawn to the dark ways.

Tonight, everything was extra quiet, much more than normal. Astrid came out here often, so he noticed things like this. He had a very complex and also intelligent mind; he could recognize ancient languages and symbols and knowledge and lore, much more than the average bird could, but more so, he had a mysterious ability.

He could see through others, especially humans, and read them as if they were mirrors. He could see their thoughts, dreams, fears, and the parts of themselves they forcefully hid, hoping no living soul would ever see. But Astrid could see it all.

After about an hour of walking in the forest, Lady Isra stopped and sat down beneath a tree and gazed thoughtfully upon the moon. She whispered to Astrid, "Why, look at that beautiful moon, what a sight to behold. Isn't nature a wonderful thing?"

Astrid replied, "Yes, and notice the beauty shines much deeper because you are here." He smiled at the witch.

That was another quality Lady Isra liked about Astrid; he always did what he could to lift her soul so high that it was almost flying away. He complimented her often and not just about beauty, but her personal beliefs, her powers, and her knowledge.

There wasn't a thing about her that Astrid did not like. Except he felt she overreacted about things; he felt like she didn't think things through properly. It was something he strongly thought, but of course, he said nothing to her as he didn't want to cause a rift between the two of them.

The witch smiled and whispered softly, "I wonder if humans fully appreciate and take time to notice the wonders of life like this, to sit here and gaze at the wonderment of it all. I hope they notice the beauty; it would be such a shame to miss it."

Astrid said nothing. He was used to Lady Isra's thoughts on humans and their mistakes; he knew she didn't like them, but he guessed she had good reason not to, so he did not judge her views on the subject. Astrid truly felt that as wicked as she was, Isra was once a sympathetic soul and in that small moment, as they sat under that tree, he saw the last piece of good that was in her. He admired it; she had thoughts and feelings like the rest, but it was only at moments like this that they emerged. She had just been wronged too often, and darkness was her way out, but again, he did not say this to her.

He knew that despite her icy heart; she had been damaged and inside was a weak girl trying to hide from it all. He had grown to love the wicked soul and so he continued being at her side, knowing that whatever she did was justified and she had good reasons for doing it.

Astrid knew she was about to do a horrible thing to Kane, and he had no care for the slave boy or what was going to happen to him. He'd seen Lady Isra had good reason, and as extreme as what she had done was, he had understood why she had killed Lillian.

Murder was an extreme way of settling a score. He trusted Lady Isra knew how extreme it was, but he also understood why it had got that far and although it wouldn't have been his way of dealing with the situation, he respected Isra and her methods and the fact it was done now, and there was no way of taking it back or changing it.

She had decided herself because that was what she wanted to do and she didn't need the help of anyone else. Even if Astrid had offered advice or suggested a way of doing things differently, there was a very good chance Lady Isra would have done it exactly how she wanted, and it would have been the same outcome.

Betrayal was something Lady Isra did not take kindly to, that he knew all too well. Astrid had come to the witch to help her and to be a friend to her. He could see how rotten she was inside, but he still wanted to be around her and play a crucial part in her life. He liked what he saw, despite how dark and evil she was.

There was a genuine goodness in her heart even though she often said she did not have one, but it was moments like this he could see her heart.

So he didn't say a word and just admired her at the moment. The two of them sat in silence for hours. The moon finally went down, the sun emerged, and Lady Isra remarked on the sun's light being in her eyes as it made her long, black curly hair glisten like shimmering black glitter.

"Come, Astrid; we best get back to beloved Kane," she said sweetly, but he knew she wasn't sweet at all. She hated the slave boy. He knew that, and he knew what was coming next, but his loyalty was to the witch, so he said nothing about it and went along with whatever she said.

They arrived back home shortly after, and Lady Isra immediately went to check on Kane. She slowly came down the stairs, quietly stood next to the door of the locked basement where Kane was trapped, and listened through the keyhole.

The slave boy was again praying for his freedom. She wanted to laugh out loud, but then remembered she had to be stealthy and quiet. She listened deeply to the boy's words as he thought he was all alone in the dark basement.

28

Kane was not aware he was being watched or listened to and held his head in his hands. and looked almost tearful as he spoke of his ordeal. He cried, "Oh, only if I had listened and just turned back when I had the chance. If only I had stayed at home with Ronald in the village, maybe I wouldn't be imprisoned against my will, and maybe I would be home with my girl."

Ronald was Kane's younger brother; they were very close and had been since childhood. Kane was the ladies man of the family and Ronald was closely following in his footsteps, but unlike Kane, Ronald was making something of his life which impressed their father. No matter what Kane did, he was the black sheep of the family.

As far as Lady Isra was concerned, Kane's fate was damned, and she was going to make it so. She continued to listen to Kane as he spoke about his situation again, unaware that the witch was listening in to him complain about his impending doom.

"Perhaps if I had stayed at home, I would be with my dear Lillian tucking into a roasted lunch with our families instead of being trapped here, faced with unspeakable evil that hates me and the entire world."

Lady Isra laughed at this remark. Unspeakable evil, she thought to herself, oh you will see evil soon enough, my boy. She tried to contain her laugh, but alas she could not. She was now cackling loudly, making it clear she had heard every single one of Kane's poor, self-pitying words. Isra was making her presence known.

Kane stopped talking as he realized the witch had heard everything. He trembled with fear as she spoke to him through the keyhole. "My boy, if you think what you have witnessed so far is unspeakable evil, then what you have to come will be absolute hell. Mark my words. You will never see happiness, or feel it in your bones again!"

She opened the door to the basement and approached the slave boy. Her piercing green eyes which were now flashing red, and she was angry, to the point she was going to explode.

He inspected her eyes as she moved toward him.

Something had changed in her; something was amiss. He was fearful and tried not to react as he could see the anger in her. They sparkled in anger and emitted a vibrant glow that shot across the room as she got closer and closer to Kane as he realized his impending fate. Kane was now fully aware he had no chance of ever escaping. He finally gave up all hope.

"Poor self-pitying boy and your pathetic ways, isn't that just so human? So glad I am not one of your kind, but you can be sure you will never get to see any of them again because when I am done here, you will know the full penalty for your betrayal, and it will be a lesson you get to live for the rest of your life." Isra retorted with a lick of satisfaction.

She locked the door behind her and returned to her tower to sit down quietly with Astrid. A thought suddenly came to her, and it made her smile as she looked at her beloved bird companion. Astrid saw the smile on her face and asked her what was making her smile.

"Tell me, lady, what is it that has made you so awash with

happiness?" Astrid asked her as he wondered why she was glowing all of a sudden.

Lady Isra answered, "I was wondering if you would like to be more involved in this than what you are? Would you like a more fulfilling role here?"

Astrid looked a little confused. He paused for a moment, then said, "I do not know what you mean. Please explain your proposition in more detail to me."

"You are a fond and most dear friend to me, and I would like to give you more than what you have now. You do not have to do anything for me anymore. Your loyalty has already been proven, but I have one last request before I set you free forever and you can leave me if that is what you wish." Isra told him explicitly.

Oh, but goodness no! Why would I leave now? I have only just got back to you. Curse the thought of it. Good golly, why would she even think such things??? Loyalty is my middle time and has been since well forever. I will never leave you, dear heart. Astrid chorused in his thoughts. He couldn't believe that Isra would think that he'd want to leave her. Isra did really befuddle him at times. She was an odd character but nevertheless it was part of her charm.

Astrid felt perplexed stammering, "But I do not wish to leave you. I will never leave you, for you are my friend."

She looked at him again and paused and went into something almost like a trance. Lady Isra thought carefully. She had grown to love and respect her raven friend, but something struck her. *Aren't I supposed to be hating the world and not capable of anything involving love or feelings?* Oh, this was a moment she had never expected, and she didn't truly know how to react.

She loved another. This was strange to her, for she had not felt love for many years. How was she going to explain this feeling? Did she even want to? She wasn't sure, but she had to answer Astrid, who was staring at her as her eyes turned back to their normal piercing green again. She was calm in his presence, and her anger had gone away.

The last time she had loved someone ie that sap Jonathan, she was burned badly, rejected, her heart ripped to pieces. And she had vowed that very day to never love again. Although it was apparent that she clearly cared for someone, and it was very weird for her and more so that she was all right with it since she expected to never find love again. She decided for now not to say a word to keep this feeling of love to herself just in case the latter would commence again.

"You don't have to. I simply wish for you to be my eyes and ears. I want to turn you into a human, but just for a little while." Isra responded coolly.

Astrid looked at her for a moment and thought about this. *A human? Hmm, life as a human, that would be interesting for a while.* He hadn't encountered many humans, nor did he care to, but this was something he was interested in doing, *if only for a short time period, to see how the other half lives. To see what makes them human. But alas I have been in this guise before it's only fitting that she deems it upon herself to transform me now. You know at times I often wonder if she truly has some of her memories because the way she mirrors with the atrocities that went on in our past is truly beguiling to me.* Astrid commented in thought, knowing that he had to answer Isra instead of stumbling around on the idea that Isra was going to make him into his former self. Oh, if only she knew.

"I accept your request. Make me a human. I feel this will be an interesting experience for both of us." Astrid replied with a glimmer of hope resounding in his eyes. It was the first time he had experienced this in twelve years.

Lady Isra smiled again and looked at her friend for the last time in his raven form. She closed her eyes and muttered some words under her breath, concentrating as she did, and after a few seconds, a black glittery mist surrounded Astrid. She continued concentrating as the mist grew bigger until she couldn't see him, and finally, she went into an intense trance.

Her head spun, and she could see pictures and shapes and colors, mainly black and grey, but as she continued to concentrate, she saw a bit of red, too. She saw herself in a graveyard, very dim, but vivid in her mind.

The pictures faded away, and she opened her eyes to see a man with hair like a raven, tall and handsome, staring right at her. It, of course, was Astrid. She looked at her friend in his new form and smiled. He was blacker than black; even his eyes were black, and she was very impressed with her work. She'd imagined all humans looked boring, but Astrid in his human form was rather dashing.

"Why, you look good. I might decide to keep you this way if you wish to be." Isra remarked in a flirtatious voice.

Astrid breathed a huge sigh of relief as he felt his new form for the first time in years. He took her hand as though it was the first time they'd met in person and replied, "If this is how you wish me to be, then this is how I will stay. My loyalty is to you and you only, and I will not break it or discard it."

She already knew he was loyal, but it was nice of him to say it to her. It was time to put him to work.

"Yes, you are loyal to me, and I do not need proof of your loyalty. Astrid, now what I wish for you is to check on the boy's family. Eliminate them if need be, but keep a watchful eye because they will try to find him. I want their efforts to be in vain." Isra instructed him carefully.

"So, you want me to find them, and if they get too close to here, you want them disposed of properly?" Astrid questioned her. He wanted to ensure he had it down correctly. The last thing he wanted to do was mess up and ruin what they were right now.

Astrid had always been a deep thinker, carefully examining every single thought to see if it was good or bad. He had a methodical mind, and he used it well, but now that the witch wanted him to monitor Kane's family, he was thinking even more. He would kill for her if needed. That was not an issue, but he wanted to make sure she was safe from the boy's family as well.

He would have to think a little more if he was to make sure of that, for he wanted nothing bad to happen to Lady Isra of the Dark.

29

strid set about his task disappearing from the warm confines of Shambre Fell but he did not let her know of his worries for her.

He paused in a moment of deep thought as he remembered the mother was already looking for Kane. She would come back again and try to seek out Lady Isra. *Perhaps someone should prevent this from happening.* Astrid mused to himself eloquently. He would take care of the mother to prevent any harm to Lady Isra, not that she needed much protection.

He reflected on the conversation that he and Lady Isra had shared before he had left, where he was clear on what he was intending to do.

Astrid turned to her. "I will go out tonight, looking around and watching for them. They will be close if they are still looking for the boy."

"You are a fine precious soul Sir Astrid. May the heavens bless you with all of the rapturous glory." Isra complimented him sweetly as he kissed her hand delicately.

"I am afraid I shall no accept no accolades. Not if my witch isn't right my side. May I just say the love and light brigade will not know what hit them because one day you and I shall rise up against the ashes and show them all what they have underestimated in both of us," Astrid pronounced with passion before he excused himself, knowing he needed to go about his next task and to do required a serious amount of finesse that only he could muster if he was to protect Lady Isra of the Dark. *It's not the first mess of hers I have cleaned up.* He chuckled sardonically to himself.

Astrid wandered the forest in his newly made human form for he found it interesting. He could walk around and feel the air with his fingers; he could feel the rain, feel the wind. He could feel everything, even feel Isra's presence, though he knew she was safely tucked away at her tower back in Shambre Fell.

Still, feeling her near him was oddly comforting. There was a connection between Isra and Astrid, and although he did not understand too much about it, he knew it was there. There was an energy between them that kept them close.

Astrid came into a wide-open space and examined it carefully. He recognized it, but couldn't work out why. It was strangely familiar to him. It was big and open, dark, and hardly any sound could be heard. An image came to his mind, an image of a dark night, a night where Lady Isra stood proudly with a dagger in her hand, belittling a human girl before stabbing her with it.

Ah, now he remembered. It was indeed the spot where Lady Isra killed Lillian, the spot where she ripped the poor battered heart out. He did not witness the killing, but he appeared just after Lady Isra was done with Lillian. His timing had been remarkable in that moment because he did not want to see Lady Isra kill anything or anyone.

He would do the killing now, as it was something he felt he had to do. It would be much better this way if he took care of it for her. Astrid was used to swooping in and discarding all trace of Isra's acts that she had enacted so it was no issue for him.

Suddenly, he wasn't alone in the forest. The open space he stood in now had a shadow in it. He turned around, and there was a massive fire behind him.

Where the hell did this come from? He thought. *Oh, there's magic in the air!*

Lady Isra was not far away; he knew that. Her presence could be felt for miles, and just how did she show herself? By putting a big fire directly behind Astrid, who knew he wasn't in any danger, but wanted to make sure he noticed her. He knew it was her because in the center of the fire, two green piercing eyes glowed at him brightly and the smoke was purple. Another of Isra's trademark colours remarking fondly on her dark purple roses that grew wildly in the garden of Shambre Fell.

Astrid took his attention away from the fire and went back to his thoughts. He needed to stay sharp for the task ahead, to eliminate the family members who were looking for Kane and, in the process, take away the limelight from Lady Isra. The mother had already met her, and even though she didn't say it, it was like she suspected Isra of something, like she just knew something wasn't right.

Of course, the witch said she had never met or seen Kane, but the mother didn't seem convinced. But what could she do? She was a human, and a weak one at that. But that was her way. All of her four children had brought her more heartache, pain, and disappointment than she could ever imagine, and every time she sat there and accepted it. She never stood up for herself and never once reprimanded any of them.

This was typical human behavior, though, typical for a woman of her age and stature to be in a family with such disrespect toward their own actions or how those actions affect others. She held the family together and kept it strong, but ultimately it did nothing because she still let all the bad things happen. Her daughter was a runaway, a drinker, a mess and again she did nothing to stop it or help, same as she had with her boys. She was a failure of a mother.

Astrid was instructed to dispose of the family members. That was her way. Isra enjoyed getting rid of things. She liked obstacles that were standing in her way to be removed and gone, so her path was clear.

Astrid's attention turned to the fire again, glowing brighter than before with its fiery orange flames and purple smoke rising to the sky as far as it could go. He had never seen purple smoke from a fire before.

Then, in between the trees, he caught sight of a figure making its way through. At first glance, he could not tell who or what it was, but then, as it came closer, he saw the figure wore a hooded cloak. He remembered where he had seen this before.

It was Kane's mother, clearly still looking for her son in the dark wilderness. Astrid saw her clearly now, and she saw him in person as he stood idly on the outskirts of Spindlevitch whereby Isra had led Lillian astray.

"Hello. I am looking for my son, Kane. He is very tall, with wavy blond hair. Have you seen him?" The woman piped up in a desperate voice.

Astrid looked at her carefully. She was worn and looked forlorn; he could see the sadness in her eyes as silent tears streamed down her tired face. She desperately missed her son and wanted him home alive. Astrid could see how much this was hurting her soul, but alas, this was not to be a reprieve; he was still going to do what needed to be done to protect the safety of Lady Isra of the Dark.

Astrid turned to the poor woman and almost pitied her. He couldn't help but feel sorry for such a poor, helpless woman who looked older than what she was. Stress and worry weighed her down and aged her greatly. He could indeed pity her, but on this occasion, he took another approach.

He quickly replied, "Hmm, Kane, eh? I believe I may have seen him. Can you tell me more about him?"

The woman began describing her son to Astrid. "He is tall, with long wavy blonde hair that goes down to his neck and he is of a well-formed build. He is my son, and he disappeared from our village a few weeks ago, and nobody has seen him since."

Astrid moved himself closer to the woman and smiled as he put his fingers to his lips and explained, "I may know where he is, but you will have to come with me as it's a place that you can only go if I am present." Astrid's wording was elusive but it was designed to be that way.

She was puzzled; she did not understand what the man she had just met in the forest said to her. It was very late in the night, and she was tired and getting more desperate as time went on. She didn't know what to do and could not think clearly. The only thing she could think of doing was to take him up on his offer and go to this place where she would be alone and in the dark with this man.

Kane's mother nodded her head and looked at Astrid. "Sure. I will go with you. I desperately need my boy home."

Astrid smiled. "Come, it is not far, and you can get a drink when we arrive. You must be terribly thirsty."

Astrid had everything well planned; he knew there was a place where humans could not be heard and had a mystical wall that only beings of magic could cross. The screams and noises the poor woman would make when she met her end would go unheard.

30

Astrid and Kane's mother walked for what seemed like many hours. They finally came to a secluded spot where there was nothing but pitch black; a dreary shadow that covered the whole place like a big black hole of misery surrounded the trees. It was dingy and dim, with no light to be seen anywhere.

He took a match out of his pocket and lit it so a plain square of earth could be seen. It was nothing fancy, didn't look mystical at all, just a plain bit of earth on the forest floor. Then he signaled for Kane's mother to stand back, holding his hand up in front of her insisting softly "There will be things occurring as a result of the magic I invoke" She nodded and did as she was told.

Concentrating on the surrounding area, Astrid closed his eyes. The earth moved. Astrid stepped back as a purple light surrounded it and sparkled like glitter evidently appearing from nowhere. It calmed down and settled for a few seconds. He seemed like he was waiting for something, but what it was, nobody knew.

Astrid paused as he looked up at the sky. Kane's mother was nervously waiting behind him and watched as he stared at the blackened sky that strangely had no moon or stars. She watched as he did what he did, using his magic very well.

She clearly did not know what was afoot. She was just taking any chance of finding her son alive. Her focus went away from her dreary thoughts as Astrid stepped back. The square glowed again, this time even more than it had done before, and suddenly a huge vortex appeared in the spot where the square was, and Astrid signaled her over.

"Come, our destination awaits. We will soon reunite you with your son."

She didn't understand magic, nor did she want to. It was unknown to her. She was a gypsy, so she knew of magic and what it was, but she knew nothing else about it. She steered clear, as she had heard many terrible stories about it.

Magic, to her, was the root of all evil. And she made sure all throughout her children's lives that they were warned to stay away from it because she wanted them safe from that dark world. There was no good there.

She'd sensed evil when she'd met Lady Isra of the Dark. If she'd had any clue or notion that her stranger was indeed Lady Isra's ally in human form, perhaps she wouldn't have been so keen to follow him on this quest to find her son.

Astrid saw she was apprehensive, so he pulled her over by her arm and dragged her into the vortex. He did not want any change in this plan. It sucked them both through this magical vortex at great speed. They saw vibrant images of color as they passed through, a buzzing sound echoing through them as they made their journey.

They arrived at their destination, a quaint little cottage deep in the woods. It was dark and perfect for Astrid's plan. It had been abandoned, so nobody would hear or see a thing that went on while they were occupying it. The outside of the cottage had a small sitting area that overlooked a once delightful border of flowers, but now they were all dead.

Whoever had lived here had not been there to look after the place for many years. It was very clear both the cottage and the garden had been neglected. The inside of the cottage was similar; the living area had a small armchair in the room's corner, and next to it was a bookcase where many books still sat unread and unloved. It was sad really, a tragedy; at one moment in time, this cottage must have been a charming home to someone.

Kane's mother reluctantly sat down on a chair while Astrid immediately went into the kitchen area to make a drink for him and his victim, or soon to be the victim, he thought wickedly.

He made up two tankards and filled both of them with water. In one, he sprinkled in some powder that became very thin and dissolved instantly. He stirred it with his finger to make sure there was no trace of it. He carefully carried the tankards into the living area and placed the tampered one into the hand of Kane's mother.

"You must be thirsty after your long journey. Here, I made this for you."

And to his amazement, she gratefully accepted it and held it to her lips to take a sip of the water. She saw Astrid looking at her, but thought nothing of it. Just a mild stare. Astrid watched her carefully and waited for her to drink the poisoned water. She felt safe and at ease, so now was a good time for this lovingly prepared gift for his tired and weary victim.

Then she drank the water. It felt refreshing at first, but then she felt her eyes getting heavy like she was about to drift off into a forceful sleep. The feeling grew stronger, and she felt her whole body becoming tired. A heavy feeling set in too and she found it hard to stay in her chair.

She felt queasy and finally closed her eyes, where she became immersed in a multidimensional world where everything was bright, and images flashed before her eyes. She was in a trance and not a very nice one. The images were powerful, flashing quickly in front of her eyes, and she trembled with some of the things she was now seeing.

She saw Kane in the witch's tower. Clear as day, she saw her son; she wanted to reach out to him, wanted to take him with her, but she couldn't, instead of floating to the next scene where she was lying on a bed. She was tied down, but of course, it was just a scary dream, wasn't it?

It felt like a dream, like she was asleep, but she also knew she was awake. She knew she was still in an armchair in the dark and abandoned cottage, and she knew Astrid was there watching the whole thing, not uttering a word.

She didn't understand why this was happening, but she knew her friend in the woods was not her friend. He just stood by and watched her as though she was a means to an end, which she was.

The woman was hallucinating. A horrible trip to Hell and back. For a gypsy like Kane's mother, it was traumatizing, as she had experienced nothing like it before. It was very new, and she hoped she would never have to do it again, but of course, she did not know that she would soon do nothing in her life again.

If it were a dream, it took a turn for the worse; next, she saw Astrid standing before her, watching her float away even deeper as she fell into a blackened hole. He was laughing at her as the nasty black hole swallowed her.

Of course, she was still sitting in the chair in the cottage, but she felt like she was in a dozen places at once. She was trying to make sense of what she saw; her son was in the witch's tower, and the mysterious lady in the woods, a witch, had her Kane captive against his will.

She tried to understand why, but then she remembered witches are the work of the devil and so he must have done something silly and against the family's beliefs in order to end up in a mess like that. It disappointed her in him but also fearful for his life and hers. Her body felt limp and weak, and she could not sit properly in the chair anymore.

She didn't comprehend what was happening and wished for it to be over. Astrid watched her as her movements became slower and her body grew weaker and weaker. After a few moments, she slumped in the chair and took one last painful breath.

Astrid checked the woman's pulse; she was dead. He admired his work with a sense of twisted pride. Now he could return to Lady Isra, as his mission had been completed. The only source of evidence to condemn Lady Isra against Kane's capture had been removed, and so wonderfully done, at that.

He checked the time on an old clock on the wall; it would be dawn soon, and he would need to leave soon in order to get back to Lady Isra's tower. He closed the dead woman's eyelids and left the cottage.

He strode off on his way and felt a cheerful sense in the air. The witch would be protected, and maybe, just maybe, she would be pleased with his efforts. She respected him like no other, but he wondered if there could be more between them. He loved her and not just as the mighty being he had grown to love and respect, but more than that. Would she ever be able to love him back?

31

Astrid walked through the main door at Shambre Fell and slowly climbed up the stairs. He heard the witch humming a blissful tune. She was in a good mood and that normally meant trouble; she was only like this when she was about to do something bad. He continued listening as he reached the top and stopped quietly by the door as he peeked through the keyhole.

She had assembled together an array of books, and next to them were potions and powders. Who knew what she was possibly up to, but she was carefully laying it out on her altar and admiring it as she placed each item in its place. He tiptoed in and greeted his friend with much sincerity.

"The deed is done. The old hag will bother you no more."

She smiled and replied, "Oh, excellent news, Astrid! It touches me deep, right here." She pointed toward her heart as she finished her remark.

She glanced back at Astrid, and asked, "So tell me, my dark friend, are you enjoying your transition as a human being, or are you disgusted with the whole miserable race?"

He spoke, and she listened with great interest to his words. "Actually, I am rather enjoying this experience."

Their conversation went on for a while before Lady Isra went out for a walk. She had some things to take care of, she'd said, but there was no clue what she had meant. Astrid had the full run of the tower and the job of monitoring the slave boy, who had not been heard from in a couple of days. He was no doubt alive; she kept him alive by feeding him and giving him water, but keeping him alive was all part of Isra's masterplan.

Astrid was just coming back from checking on Kane in the basement when he heard a strange sound coming from upstairs. He rushed there and opened the door, but couldn't see anything. A tapping sound came from the window.

He opened the window to see what the noise was and noticed a small owl perched on the windowsill. It was staring at him dead in the face, then flew off as if for Astrid to follow it. Astrid immediately ran down the long staircase and ventured out into the grounds. The owl was perched on the wall next to him, and it flew off again, signaling him to follow.

Slowly following the owl, Astrid went out in the forest, following the owl until it came to a gigantic oak tree and stopped. Astrid paused and wondered why it had stopped; he saw a green snake fast asleep at the top of the tree. He could only just see it as the tree was tall, but clear as day, there was the green snake which he recognized as Romeo, the friend of Lady Isra.

Then he noticed the owl had sat down beside the tree and was looking up. Astrid couldn't quite make out what the owl was looking at; he saw the snake wasn't asleep. He was dead. Green slime dripped down the tree branches, and he thought for a moment about how he would tell Lady Isra about this tragic event, but then he saw something else. Someone had stabbed Romeo with a magical dagger with a note attached to it that Astrid couldn't see.

Astrid kindly asked the owl, "Can you please fetch that note for me? I would like to know what is on it."

The owl obliged and flew up to Romeo's dead body. Carefully, he scooped up the note in its beak, flew back down and dropped it in

Astrid's hand. It was tattered and looked like it had been there for several days.

It read: "You told the witch's slave boy what she was; now you have paid the price. Goodbye, Sir Romeo."

It dawned on Astrid that Romeo's death wasn't a random killing, but again he read the note to himself, scanning the words carefully as he did so. Romeo must have betrayed Lady Isra.

Not only had the snake been brutally stabbed and killed, but he had betrayed Lady Isra by revealing to Kane something about her. It was something that could have compromised the plan of Kane's demise and also Lady Isra's safety. That was the part he was more concerned about.

He turned around to thank the owl, but it had gone. Completely disappeared. He decided he would take the note back to Lady Isra's tower and somehow break the news to her that not only had her friend been killed but that he had indeed betrayed her. This wouldn't be something she would enjoy hearing. Of course, she hated being betrayed. He placed the tattered note in his pocket and left the scene, taking care to make sure nobody saw him.

KANE WAS IN HIS DINGY, dark basement. It was like a cell. Since his last encounter with Lady Isra, he had no longer been forced to do chores; he was now permanently locked in the basement, whereas before he had the run of the whole tower. Lady Isra had decided that this was the best way of keeping him under her total control.

A bowl of berries was lying on the floor next to him; he couldn't trust if they were safe to eat or not. Kane thought they may well have been poisoned, so he sat on the cold floor, looking weary and forlorn. He knew he was no longer a slave, but just a prisoner, and that was enough to keep him thinking dark, depressing thoughts.

What would happen to him? Would he die? Or perhaps, somehow, he would escape, but he seriously doubted that would happen as he knew Lady Isra had him on lockdown for a purpose. Setting eyes on Lady Isra would be a mistake he would never forget, but he had no clue of what was coming to him, other than he was in deep trouble.

Alas, it was his own fault for seeking the witch, for failing to be a strong man, and for being too greedy in wanting more than what he had. He was the only one to blame for his troubles and misfortune of being in his jail cell. He wished sometimes he could turn the clock back, but now was no time for such self-pitying thoughts. The deed was done. Being alone with his regrets was even worse than being Isra's prisoner.

ASTRID WAS BACK and sat in the witch's tower, waiting for her to come home after her walk. He had a lot to tell her, and he wasn't sure how she was going to react to it all.

Astrid hoped she would be calm and would see the positive side, but he knew what she was like.

32

His thoughts about what Lady Isra might have thought about all this stopped in their tracks when he heard a door slam and footsteps approaching. They were fast and loud; the main door swung open, and Lady Isra walked in. But she did not look happy. She looked anything but happy.

Astrid was about to ask what was wrong when, without warning; she threw a potion bottle against the wall and it smashed, splattering its contents everywhere. Astrid looked confused and worried. Isra's hands shook as she saw what she had done, the liquid a shade of dark blue dripping from the walls and making a toxic smell as it hit the floor.

She finally spoke. "I've just been to the forest, and I ventured into the clearing where I normally go on my long walks to think. There was an owl there; it seemed it had followed me all the way."

Astrid tried to act surprised. Isra continued, trying to calm her voice. "It said someone or something that I would kill him warned that Kane. So, someone has betrayed me. But the owl did not wish to tell me who my betrayer is, despite my desire to know their identity."

Ah, she did not know who it was; therefore, she didn't know about

Romeo. The owl had refused to disclose that information. Astrid thought for a moment about this latest addition to the puzzle and decided he would not tell Isra about Romeo. She clearly didn't know that he was dead, as surely, she would have mentioned that part, so he decided she did not need to know.

He replied, "Well, I wouldn't worry yourself with that too much, as we have Kane locked in the basement and shall continue to keep him there until you decide what you wish to do with him."

She sat down beside Astrid, took his hand while smiling and said, "Thank you, dear Astrid, your words are such a comfort to me. You have been so loyal and dedicated to me. Thank you." She suddenly thought about Kane. "So how is the whimpering mess of a human today?"

Astrid laughed and replied to her, "Kane is fine. He left his berries. He said he didn't want them as he thought you may have poisoned them."

She seemed to find this hilariously funny and sneered. "No such luck for that poor mortal. I want him alive, not dead."

She wanted him to be breathing when the time came. This showed just how much she wanted to punish him and how cruel she was planning to be for the right time to do so.

And that time was not far away.

Isra taunted him more and more as she knew it was coming closer to the day she would show him his prize, when she would reveal Lillian laying on the forest floor as she had been for many weeks now. It was to be the main event of her revenge that she was going to serve him.

He did not know what was headed his way except that he was in big trouble and that he would never leave. He had a sinking feeling he was never getting away from the witch's grasp, but he didn't know of all the lovely fun things that were in store for him. That was going to be Lady Isra's big surprise.

She laughed again, and Astrid replied, "I think he knows you want him alive. He knows deep down in his human soul that this is going to be the way of things for a reason, not a coincidence."

He had been down to visit the slave boy a few times and sussed the young Kane out. Astrid hadn't been here for very long, probably a few months, but during his time Kane had been the big fixture in the dwelling of Lady Isra. Why?

He needed little time to question this. She wanted revenge on him; she wanted him to pay, and after getting to know the witch, he knew this was how she worked with anything and anyone who got on the wrong side of her. If they were lucky enough to tell the tale, they'd never make that same mistake again; he knew that much.

With Kane, it was a case of sheer blindness, from what Astrid could see, because he had a good life, but he was foolish enough to throw it all away for something tempting, something different, something wicked; Lady Isra.

It was clear to Astrid that Kane had a crush on the witch. It was almost like he was in awe of her, like she was the most wonderful sight to be admired that he had ever seen. Like she was some wonderful thing to possess and take control of but had he a bit more hindsight, he would have known that something like control with Lady Isra would never have worked, so oddly enough he didn't get his wish.

He sought her because he wanted women to fall over themselves for him. It must have struck a nerve in Lady Isra, as she hated being used for selfish human gains and so she punished him. The rest was quite clear to Astrid, and in his eyes, the witch had done nothing wrong. He also guessed Kane may have had other ideas for Lady Isra, but she would never have been interested in those "ideas" even if he had proposed them to her.

Kane may have wanted her sexually, but that wouldn't have gone over well with her at all. She hated humans, and he was pretty sure that even though he was currently a human, she could never be with one, let alone get along with one. With Astrid, it was only because he knew Lady Isra saw him as a being, and not a human.

He respected her for that. He was enjoying his change as a human for now, but he knew what he truly was, and so did she. Even though he was currently in human form; Astrid wasn't acting like one; he wasn't talking like one or behaving like one. Astrid was a magical being with intelligence, knowledge and caring, and he was positive in his outlook on life. Astrid also prided himself in being kind to others.

Astrid always wanted to help people and beings, no matter what the situation was, and even if the person or being didn't truly deserve the help, he still offered it. That was one of his greatest strengths. Lady Isra was even a little in love with this part of him, the way he loved to help because that kind of kindness and caring had never been bestowed upon her.

She did care once, sure she did, but every time she had, it was never appreciated and sometimes, never wanted. One day, she just stopped caring. It's sad, but her turn was a slow process; she wasn't always wicked; you know.

Lady Isra finally said, "Well, he won't need to be kept here for much longer. Time is short and his day is coming." She finished with a smile.

It was at this moment Astrid suddenly felt something spark in him. Kane's demise would come soon, so he should tell Lady Isra how he felt about her. Even if it turned out, she didn't feel the same way back.

What harm could it do? Astrid thought to himself as he studied her for a moment, her piercing green eyes glowing at him as she admired his black eyes staring back at her. He then said, "I think I need to go for a walk, just to get some fresh air for a moment or two." He turned to leave, but waited for her to respond.

She replied, "Okay, but don't be long. You know I need you here."

That was it. She needed him. Those were the most crucial words she could have said at that moment. **You know I need you here.**

He repeated her words over and over in his mind, making sure he had heard them correctly, but of course, he had. She said she needed him. He pondered while staring at the moon; it was awfully bright.

At first, he thought it may have been a sign that even in the darkest of places, there could still be a shining, strong, and empowering light. In the darkest pits of her soul, she needed someone else; *surely this was not a characteristic of someone who was pure evil?* Or maybe it was, and she found something in him that sparked some light in her. Again, it was like a part of her had remembered him from their time before but she had no comprehension as to how.

It was a bit of a shock, too much of a shock if he were being honest. A good shock, though. Being needed was always good, and with that, he looked at the moon one more time and ventured back into the tower of Lady Isra of the Dark.

She was waiting on the floor where she had been before he went out. "Pleasant walk?" she inquired.

"Yes, actually."

Her eyes sparkled at his, and a very tiny glow of red appeared at the base of her heart. It had never been there before, but he saw it now. It was deep, blood red, and glowing brightly like the reddest ruby.

He continued to speak. "I have been thinking. We have grown very close during my time here, and I was wondering if it could be more than what we have? Could there be something other than a powerful friendship between us?"

She didn't know what to say. This was something she had not expected to come from the raven turned man's lips. She was curious and also flattered; curious to see where this could go, flattered because someone was interested in her for just her alone. No hidden agendas, no shifty tricks. Astrid was invested in her.

She looked at him and replied, "Well, my dear Astrid, what do you mean? Is it you want us to be lovers?" She felt brave asking but asked, anyway.

He straightened himself for a moment and looked back at her. "Yes. But do you want to be with me? Could you see us being strong for eternity?"

She answered him with a smile, "I think we could. I don't know anyone else who could get me like you do, and I love the dark things we share. Yes, I feel we could be."

Astrid looked thrilled; he pulled himself close to her and

whispered while breathing against her neck, "I think I want to do this."

And with that, he kissed her so passionately she didn't know what to do other than kiss him back. It was powerful; the energies between them unified, and it was so intense that neither of them realized what was happening until the moment the kiss ended.

33

The next morning at the tower, things were very different. For the first time in years, Lady Isra had a companion, and she had slept in his arms all night long. It was a defining moment where she'd felt safe and warm for the first time in many moons. They awoke very early, still entwined in one another and wrapped in the sheets on her bed.

She awakened first as she was used to waking early, but as she had Astrid by her side now, nuzzling her as she woke. The warm sunlight showered them both as they laid in each other's arms, blissfully unaware that day had broken until it became so bright through the windows they realized the sun was out and coming through to start the day. She felt a new lease on life in herself as she snuggled up to her lover.

Astrid and Isra were not naked and had not been together sexually, but they had been in each other's arms all night, and it was a deep, powerful connection that they shared while romanticizing beautiful thoughts to one another. They were so happy; they had almost forgotten that Kane was holed in the basement.

She nudged him and sweetly said, "You haven't been to check on the boy today. We've been up here so long, who knows how much time we have lost." She realized she had never been this happy in such a long time.

Astrid tightened his grip around her and whispered, "He will live, it won't kill him to starve for a few hours. For one day this man Kane will not be the main event in this household." He pulled her closer to him as they laid snuggled up to each other.

She let herself fall from his grip a little and said, "The time is coming soon where he will be a fixture no more, and you know what that means. I will need you at my side when that time is here, but it won't be long."

He listened to her and gently asked, "It won't be long? It won't be long until what?"

She looked at him dead in the face and honestly replied, "His comeuppance has been delicately wrapped, and now it's almost time for him to open it."

Astrid then forced his gaze on her again and asked, "Are you going to kill him?"

He waited for her answer, but she just looked at him; no reply, no response. Just a mild stare, and with that, he gripped her again, and she allowed him to pull her close. She wanted to reassure him; he felt worried that she could tell, but Astrid had nothing to worry about. There was nothing that could go wrong, as it had been perfectly planned.

What must have been laying in the back of Astrid's mind was, *what if something goes wrong with Kane? Supposing he does something to Isra? What if it goes to hell and what if he loses her?* He seemed worried for her, worried that she was going too far. Also extremely anxious that something could happen to her. He wanted more than ever to keep her safe and away from harm as he did right now in this moment.

These thoughts lasted for a few minutes, and then he kissed her neck and the moment of worry faded. They decided they would get on with their day as they usually would, but this time, united as one, as they were in their own form of special magic.

Astrid went down to the basement to check on Kane and peeked through the keyhole and saw he was asleep. *See?* he thought to himself. *No need to worry about him today. He doesn't need to be in our lives.* He walked past again and went back upstairs.

Lady Isra was in deep thought mode; she was trying to collect herself, focusing on a calm state with her eyes closed while sitting up as she had one hand held on each side of a crystal ball.

She was trying to communicate with someone or something, but at this stage, it was hard to tell which.

She was distracted by Astrid coming into the room, so the mood passed. He saw how hard she was trying, so he stood behind her and gently placed her hands on both sides of the crystal ball again and whispered, "Give it one more try."

So, with Astrid's support, she did again and focused while allowing him to give her strength. There was a strong and vibrant light emitting from the pair of them that was red and also deep purple. It was as bright as anything could be for two dark beings, but she could get in the zone and images were forming inside the crystal ball.

She was trying to get a clear view, but most of it appeared hazy. She thought she could see a creature, but it turned out to be the ocean, which she found odd, as there were no oceans nearby. Then a message came to her about something in the past, or was it the past?

She wasn't sure, so she continued. It said, "Something needs to be left in the past," and she didn't understand this so went back to the ocean part and then saw herself standing near an ocean, ready to let go of something.

Ah, so something needs to be left in the past, she thought to herself, but what? She wasn't the "letting go" type, so being told she needed to let go of something wasn't that much of a propitious moment, but she listened to the words and let the images flow.

She thought it could be to do with Kane; perhaps it was about letting her grudge with him go, but she wasn't about to do that. No, he was a pathetic human, and he was going to pay for his mistakes, no matter what messages the higher powers sent to her saying otherwise. She had already decided in her mind that this was going to happen and she knew he deserved to be punished. He needed to learn that it was not okay to piss her off; in her mind, she was justified about the entire thing.

The dark hours soon came, so Astrid took her away from the crystal ball and her thoughts and they retired for the night, despite her never wanting to sleep. She wasn't much of a sleeper, but that night she slept comfortably and was silent all night. Not a single thing disturbed her.

The night after many hours turned to morning, and it was a beautiful morning.

34

Finally, the sunlit day that had been longed for came. The sun streamed through the blackened window frames of Lady Isra's tower as it glistened like flames of fire. Today was the day that Isra had been preparing for months. It was time to show Kane just what the price was for betraying a witch. It was finally time to show him what she'd been long awaiting to.

Would she give him a chance to explain himself for his betrayal, or would she go all the way? There wasn't much left to do now; it was time to bring the whimpering slave boy to his doom. Astrid had carefully murdered the boy's mother, and everything had been well prepared. Now there was only one thing to do: drag him out of his dreary basement cell.

Isra sent Astrid to get Kane out of his jail cell as she prepared herself for today's events. Isra even wore the black dress that she had worn when she'd killed Lillian. Isra admired herself in the mirror, briefly tousling her black curls, then went downstairs to wait for Astrid.

It was finally time.

Astrid was waiting outside with Kane and had already told him to wait for the witch to arrive, as she would instruct him what he had to do.

Kane looked confused and didn't understand. "What is going on? Is she going to free me?"

Astrid looked at him and replied, "It is not up to me. You know you played your own part in this, and now she wants to do her part. You will find out soon."

Isra strode out of the door, looking powerfully amazing in her black lace dress. She had worn it, as she felt it was special. It had feeling and memory to it and was significant to today's events. Lady Isra walked up to Astrid and planted a kiss on his cheek, and then turned her attention to Kane.

As she admired him looking scared, she softly said, "Today's the day, and boy, do I have the most wonderful thing in store for you, my dear." Then she turned to Astrid and smiled as she said, "I will need you later."

Kane got angry at this point and blurted out his frustration and fears. "You need him? But more to the point, do you think he needs you? You are a twisted bitch, no man on this earth needs you."

Lady Isra laughed. She found his outrage amusing and then smiled, turning to Astrid again, "Well, if that is the case, he would not be here, but it is no matter. I will consult Romeo when I return."

At this moment, both Kane's and Astrid's faces dropped. Astrid looked at her and said calmly, "Romeo is dead."

"Oh," she replied, a little in shock and then looked at Astrid as she said, "Well then, I guess we best get on with things since there is nothing left to do."

Astrid thought she may be upset, not just about Romeo's death, but about his knowledge of it. But she seemed okay. She was strong and continued with what she was doing. She stood, smoothed out her dress and began to address Kane.

"It is time. Your future awaits you. Come, we must go. Now."

He appeared to be shaking all over. She took his hand and dragged him away with her. He didn't want to go; he was scared, there was no doubt of that, but he had no choice but to follow her. They walked for many miles; they went down many dark roads, and she continued to drag him even though he felt weary and scared of what was ahead.

She knew what was ahead, but he didn't but still off they went, further and further until there was no turning back and they were at the center of the forest, it was still light, and she kept her tight grip on Kane's hand forcefully as she dragged him closer and closer to what looked like an open plan area.

They were minutes away from where the corpse of Lillian was to be found.

35

She continued holding his hand as they got closer to the place she had planned for them to be, and then she suddenly let go of it. He didn't understand why, but he took a step backward as he tried to familiarize himself with the location. The air was clear, and the sun was shining, cascading its warm rays over them as Kane continued trying to understand his surroundings.

Isra flashed him a shy smile and said, "We are not here to enjoy the view, but I am glad you like it."

She continued and smiled again as she looked to the center. There laid Lillian, dressed in white with roses wrapped around her, and in her hair. All over her were splatters of dried blood the color of rust.

She looked at Kane and said, "Look! Look what is here for you."

And he looked. He saw nothing of importance at first; he didn't understand what it was he was supposed to be looking at. Then he saw her. He let out a small scream, and his eyes bulged.

This was the girl he had planned to marry someday, and here she was, dead and carefully decorated in the center of the forest. She looked so peaceful and so beautiful; he suddenly remembered why he was attracted to her, but it was too late now. She couldn't hear his words or feel his thoughts. They fell on deaf ears.

Lady Isra carefully noted his reaction, but before he could speak, she stopped him. "You tried to betray me, you tried to take something that was not yours, and now you pay the price. There your dear Lillian lies; she has been waiting for you."

He was suddenly dumbfounded and couldn't speak or move. He was in shock. There, right in front of him, was everything he had ever loved and had now lost. He could not comprehend what was happening, but he knew it was very real.

Lady Isra smiled and continued. "She bled beautifully for a small girl." she said wickedly as she showed him how Lillian's decomposed body, a mark of what happened that day. But she wasn't done with him yet.

Isra slowly watched as he stared at her and then stared at Lillian, unable to keep his eyes off both but yet impossible to look at them both at the same time. He was so full of despair he didn't know where to look.

His reaction immensely pleased her and continued her taunting of him. "I told her what you had done, how you left her to seek something more. She didn't cry out for you or beg you to save her, but I watched her little human heart sink as she realized what had been done to her and the betrayal in her heart killed her alone."

Kane felt very sick and very disoriented. He wasn't being killed; he wasn't being told to beg for his life. This was something much worse, and he could never have envisioned this in his wildest of dreams and perhaps some of his nightmares.

Still, Isra continued; she walked right up to him and smiled wickedly as she whispered, "My dagger played a small part, but it was you who broke her heart and this, my friend, is something you will live with for all eternity."

He looked at her for the first time since hearing about Lillian's murder, and he wanted to get away from her as fast as he could, but something in him didn't allow it. He could not move and continued listening.

"This day will stand still in your mind and embody your soul for many years to come."

He became defeated by her wicked and cruel words. But they were the truth, and that is what he hated most. She was telling him what he indeed was.

"But you know this. You know what you are, and you know what you have done."

He was now on his knees with his head in his hands. She could have done anything to him; she could have tortured him, cut off his limbs and dangled them on a string and he wouldn't have cared. He just so badly wanted this to be over.

Kane was in luck, as Isra was almost done. Isra had done what she had set out to do. She had slowly destroyed a man's soul at the very core in a matter of minutes. She was pleased.

She then walked up to the boy and kissed his cheek as she wiped a tear from his deep blue eyes and whispered to him, "You will remember me for the rest of your life, but there is nothing you can do about it. Now you are free to go."

The scene then faded, like a dead memory lingering on in the winds.

As time grew on, the day turned to night, and the rain came down heavily. There was no clue what happened to Kane, whether he had run for his life or stayed holding onto what was left of his beloved dead bride in the center of the forest. Perhaps he had run and perhaps he had learned his lesson, but nobody knew.

He might have still been alive, and if so, he was most likely living with his deep pain burdening his soul over everything he had lost at the hands of a witch and a mistake he would never make again.

Lady Isra disappeared after those last words to Kane at the scene of Lillian's body, and she was not seen again, but for quite a while, her tower was still visible and so was Astrid, the raven who still lingered. But no Lady Isra. She was nowhere to be seen.

It formed many questions following the disappearance of Lady Isra of The Dark. Why weren't Lady Isra and Astrid together? Had he had his heart broken by her? Was she still lurking around somewhere?

Not a single soul knew, and they couldn't find her nor any answers about her in the deep mystery that surrounded her and her legacy.

A few months later, on a warm summer day, the tower completely disappeared, but on the very grounds in which it had once stood, quietly perched on a tree branch was Astrid, the raven. He was still there, even though she and her dwelling were long gone.

But was she gone? Perhaps she had just cloaked herself and her dwelling further so the human eye could not see. Maybe she would reemerge one day and return, but again, nobody knew what had happened, and it was all a bit of mystery and a legend.

Astrid, her faithful lover, could always be seen in that very spot where she had once been, and he was still there watching, so maybe she was there, but nobody knew if she would return to her rightful place by his side.

But, for now, all that remains is the legend that once was.

The End

INTRODUCING HER DARK HEART

DARK SPELL SERIES BOOK 6

It was on a summer night with pink darkened skies, just after dusk, that a raven flew in from beneath the clouds and landed on the grassy bank, in the middle of a great forest. At first glance, it was just a raven, one as you would expect it to be, with beady black eyes that held the tiniest hint of yellow and beautifully blackened wings.

But a moment later, you would realize this raven was not just any raven; his form shifted to that of a man. The man admired his handsome appearance and muttered under his breath a few choice words, unheard by humans, just as he wanted.

This raven, now transformed into a man, was Astrid, the faithful lover of Lady Isra; she was the witch who dwelled in the forest.

A year ago, her tower disappeared from view. Astrid had insisted on this as a very important security measure. He was determined to shield the witch from human eyes and wanted to maximize her safety. But of course, she was more than capable of looking after herself, being a witch and all.

He and Lady Isra had been together for about a year and a half now, and they were very close companions. He loved the dark heart inside the witch and was very fond of her, as she was of him. Any time he went out, he would transform into his raven form.

The reason he was so careful when he ventured in and out was that Lady Isra and Astrid's tower had been cloaked from all human eyes with a powerful invisibility spell, and only a few specially chosen words made it visible. It worked the same way as a door, and only he and Lady Isra had the metaphysical key that opened the dark fortress that was their home.

A few things had changed in the tower since Astrid had been with Lady Isra; the interior had changed slightly. He preferred the color red, and it dominated most of the building. He liked the vibrant energy it gave off, so it was the focus of their home. Their bedroom was a combination of purple, red, and black with a black bed covered with the bedspread and matching curtains around it, showcasing purple and black walls. All of this, as if done by magic.

Astrid had become an expert at transforming since he had become somewhat human in his form, although in reality, not human. It was just a body, and he never saw himself as a human. He had learned how to work and manage his energy better and also worked with Lady Isra on a lot of her spells. She had taught him much, and he was a fast learner, as he didn't need a single tool to work his magic!

Not just any old raven could do these things. Lady Isra was proud of how outstanding he had become. This was a very creative and also visual gift, and not just for anyone. Astrid had mastered this well, and although he struggled with reading, he had completed the study quickly and had accomplished a lot.

But what about Lady Isra? What about her powers, you might say?

Had they grown or weakened? Well, neither. Since her revenge on Kane, she found she didn't need to use magic, but this was also because of Astrid's presence. She had found her other half, and she was complete now. Still dark, but not needing to use magic. However, if something arose, then of course she would deal with it, magically.

And before you say it, no, she had not turned over a new leaf.

When you are dark, you are dark. You don't go back. Lady Isra had no intention of going back; she wasn't about to become some goody two shoes that would go dancing off into the light. No, that would be rather boring, wouldn't it? Her need to use magic had just lessened; that was all.

Since getting her revenge and destroying Kane, she didn't find she had a need for magic. The impulses and the power it gave her were still there, but she didn't need it. Whether you would consider that good or bad would be at your discretion, and I will allow you to make your judgements on that. Lady Isra was quite happy with it all.

She looked radiant. Her long black curly hair was now down to her bottom, and her piercing green eyes even greener, as if it brightened them with lightning.

But what other changes were there around the place, I hear you say?

Astrid and Lady Isra were as strong as they could ever be in their union filled with power, love, trust and their loyalty that was as solid as the walls of the tower themselves. Nothing could ever break it down or tear it, it was that mighty and powerful force to be reckoned with as it seemed nothing could destroy or interfere with the energy and power that was between them.

After Kane's demise, it was Astrid who had ordered the tower be cloaked from the human world so Lady Isra could be protected. It was not clear why he had wanted this, but her location and the fact she was still around were to remain a closely guarded secret. It was all his doing; it was what Astrid had insisted on.

Lady Isra had no part in it except that she agreed to his request as she was honored at how much he cared about her safety and wellbeing. Nobody except Astrid and Lady Isra would have any clue over its existence; humans could not find it, and magical folk would have an equally hard time as it was so well hidden.

Astrid paused for a moment as he felt an energy go through him and then he stepped inside. It was quiet, but he called for Lady Isra to see if she was home. He was very cautious about her going out, but alas, she was a free spirit, and he could not always guarantee what he said would be ordered.

He made it clear he didn't do this to control her, but he was very protective of the witch's well being. He showed this by the way he shouted her name, "ISRA!" Not angrily, but there was a forceful tone in his voice all the same.

She heard him and promptly revealed herself to him, letting him place a kiss on her forehead as a sign of love and protection, showing devotion to another. Something that Lady Isra had not experienced for a very long time until meeting Astrid.

"Good morning, I trust all is well in that ghastly human world?" she joked as he placed his hands around her neck, drifting down toward her chest and embracing her.

"Yes, they are fine, still so terribly human."

She laughed at this for a moment and then paused as she heard noises that sounded like they were coming from outside. Astrid heard it too as he saw her eyes dart to the window.

"What was that?" she asked, looking at him for some validation.

He sternly replied, "I do not know, but I hope for their sake, they know who I am."

She thought to herself, Well, they may not, but I know who you are.

He got up, along with her, and went to the window to see what it was. Now, of course, with the tower being cloaked, when she looked out of the window to see what it was she could see out, but they could not see her. That is how strong the cloaking of the invisibility spell was, to make sure that nobody outside of the protective cloak could see in or get in.

A very strong and good solid way of protecting their home and Lady Isra, he wasn't too bothered. As who would dare enter the home of a witch? Not forgetting a raven hidden under the guise of a man who was always in her presence. He had strong, prominent abilities that could harm anyone who threatened Isra, if he truly felt the need to. But whoever it was, in his mind, they clearly had a death wish.

He looked out of the window, and much to the surprise of Lady Isra, dashed downstairs and went into the grounds of the tower. Something had spooked him, but it was not clear what.

He dashed down the stairs like fire.

DARK SPELLS READING ORDER

1. Her Dark Love
2. Kissing Darkness
3. Seducing Darkness
4. Queen of Darkness
5. Her Dark Soul
6. Her Dark Heart
7. Her Dark Rose
8. Darkness Reborn

ABOUT THE AUTHOR

USA Today Best Seller Isra Sravenheart resides in the UK. She is an avid reader, particularly in the fantasy and paranormal genres, and very much into all things fairytale and dark in nature. She is also a witty wordsmith.

Isra is known for being obsessed with coffee and very particular towards cats of which she owns four of the buggers.

You can follow Isra through her blog, or any of these social media platforms:

ALSO BY ISRA SRAVENHEART

The Dark Spell Series: Books 1 through 8

Heart of Oz

Tainted Siren

The Divine Spiritual Truth: A Twinflame Romance